A powerful story of trust . . .

Journey

on

Rural Roads

BOOKS BY KATHY MCCRAY

JOURNEY TO FORGIVENESS
JOURNEY TO PINE STREET
CREATIVE CUTBACKS GUIDELINES TO RIGHTEOUS
LIVING

Visit the Kathy's Pen Web Site at:
http://www.kathyspen.com

JOURNEY
ON
RURAL
ROADS

Kathy McCray

Newport News, Virginia, USA

Published by
Kathy's Pen

This novel is a work of fiction. Names, characters, places, and incidents either are the product of the author's imagination or are used fictitiously.

Scripture quotations marked (NIV) are taken from the HOLY BIBLE, NEW INTERNATIONAL VERSION ®.NIV ®.
Copyright © 1973, 1978, 1984 by International Bible Society. Used by permission of Zondervan. All rights reserved.

ISBN: 0-9777034-2-8

Printed in the United States of America

Pass the test and have it all!

Chapter 1

Vanessa you're fired!" The word "fired" kept ringing in her head over and over.

A cold sweat fell upon her entire body as a police officer guided her off the business premises. Humiliation swelled as she went by her colleagues as they murmured, knowing what had happened to her. Her head hung low because it was too painful to hold it up. She felt disgusted and wobbly as she grasped her purse in one hand and the three pictures of her kids in the other. She marched with speed so that the officer had to step up his stride to keep up with her. Outside the high-rise building, she was in a trance. It took her a couple of minutes to think of where she had put her car. And then, spotting it, she strode even quicker than she had on the inside. As she tried to unlock her car door, her hands were shaking. She dropped the keys, and the officer kindly picked them up. He opened her car door for her, and said, "Life is horrible at times." She uttered not a word.

As she sat in her car, she was hurt. The word "fired" kept ringing in her ears. She sensed a sharp pain in her breast, and tasted the saltiness of her tears as they automatically began to drizzle down her cherry colored face. She tried to find a tissue as the officer got in his automobile and pulled up alongside her, waiting to accompany her outside the security gate. She said to herself, "Nothing is going right in my life, and I can't even find a tissue." Since she was unable to find one, she used her blouse to wipe her face and runny nose.

"Why?" she asked as she secured the steering wheel. "In absolute truth, I need my job because of the three small mouths I have to feed. How am I going to survive? I have nowhere to go and no one to turn to," she cried aloud.

She felt as though giving up was the best option since her life was spiraling downward right before her eyes. She tried to put the key in the ignition, but it wouldn't fit. It was as if she was putting the pieces of a puzzle together. At last, she got the key in the ignition, but as she turned it, it failed. Her hands were trembling furiously. Her shout got louder as she said, "I'm going to do this," and it started on the fourth try.

She wanted time to revert to the fantastic early morning sunrise experience that she had had before work. She had awakened joyful and early to view the sunrise, because it meant a lot to her on her twenty-fifth birthday. The onset of sunshine produced an intensive sense of hope and amazing possibilities as she ignited two candles on the marble tub, and soaked in the hot bubble bath for almost an hour. As she soaked, she felt the radiation of the magical sunshine over shadowing her sunset environment of everyday struggles, misfortunes, and distresses. The precious time to herself generously helped restore the brokenness in her life temporarily by allowing her to ignore her unresolved problems.

The officer was tolerant as he waited for her to go, and it was evident that it was no turning back for her. This wasn't a distant dream, but a virtual reality. The emotional pain that she experienced she wouldn't wish on her worst enemy. Had she deserved firing or been a horrible employee maybe it wouldn't have felt as bad. But the opposite was true. She was one of a handful of the productive employees working for the company. "Why did this travesty have to occur?" she said, as the tears relentlessly continued to roll down her face.

Once outside the technology gate she started to travel on the familiar road, but now it appeared alien to her. She was lost in her sorrows and the bumpy terrain. She had a whim she would never recoup.

Still weeping she chanted, "Happy birthday to me, happy birthday to me," and continued with, "what an excellent gift to unexpectedly receive." She never imagined her beautiful morning would wind up on a sour note, but it had.

Her journey appeared endless. Her attention wasn't on her driving. It was evident when she ran off the roadway two times and rushed passed a red light, a lapse that almost caused her to strike a red convertible. The norm typically was to pick her kids up from daycare before she proceeded home. But it was different as she looked in the rear-view mirror at her pale, yet crimson cheeks and her tear-stained face. She didn't stop. She desired time to think and rid herself of the stress before she cared for them.

As she entered the main entranceway door to her apartment, she spotted a notice affixed to her front door. She read, "By the Pine City Court, you are hereby ordered to vacate the premises no later than one week from today." She forcefully pulled the notice off the doorway and dropped her keys unintentionally. After grabbing them from the cement floor, she opened her apartment door and slammed it shut. She sped to her room and barged into her pillow on her neatly made bed as she cried.

She started to yell out, "This can't be taking place, not on the same day. Fired! Evicted! No! No! What am I to do? I don't see the sunrise for the sunset." For hours, she cried over the fairytale dreams she had had that never happened, for her pathetic man who rejected his obligations as a father or a devoted husband, and for her inadequacy to help herself or her kids. She was in a predicament and considered taking her own life to evade the shipwreck. But as she thought about her kids being alone and having no one to care for them, she reassessed her madness.

Vanessa Hawkins was a small, medium framed, intelligent Caucasian woman. She dressed homely and wore her dresses below the knee. She smiled a lot, despite the sunset in her life. Today was different because the sunset had overshadowed her. She often wondered why life couldn't be different and why the sunlight couldn't shine forever. She didn't want the sunset, but it oftentimes would find her and consume all her sunlight hours.

As she relaxed on her bed still embracing her cushioned pillow, she thought about her seven-year marriage to Steven Hawkins, her high school sweetheart. It was a total failure. They had married a month before she had graduated from high school and lived together for almost one year when he said he felt trapped after the first baby came. Their daughter Jasmine was now six years old. He accused Vanessa for getting pregnant against his will. He thought he wasn't old enough to have kids.

To date, they were separated for six years. They had been intimate twice since the separation, and each time she wound up pregnant, first with Jackie, her three-year-old, and second, with Eric her eight month old. She loved her three kids because they were her light, but she was dissatisfied in how Steven had turned against those that appreciated him most. He blamed it on his mother for getting married three times and having the numerous male friends. This taught him that men either ran around on females or didn't hang around very long. Therefore, he desired freedom to come and go as he pleased to avoid this death sentence he called "marriage." He thought it was too much responsibility, but Vanessa called it growing up.

He pursued his own aspirations in his hometown of Mary, Virginia, thirty minutes away from her. With the help of one of his cousins, he had acquired a good paying job as manager of a local grocery store. He refused to help her out financially with the kids. He would come to visit and whenever he left, he would place five or ten dollars on the table. He had discussed divorce, but she was against it because of her upbringing in a two-parent home. She wanted the same for her children. She told him that she would never divorce, but would wait until he discovered what was important, even if it took a lifetime. His importance was several female companions at a time with no commitment, fancy clothes, a party life, and nice vehicles.

She had anger toward him that had turned to hatred during the last winter season when she lacked money to buy Eric a coat. The last time she saw him, he had on a trendy navy blue two-piece suit and peach shirt with a matching colorful designer tie. His sharpness flowed all the way down to the navy blue socks he was wearing with his black snakeskin shoes. He looked as though he'd come out of a male fashion magazine, but he was useless to her and her kids. She was to the point that whenever anyone asked about him or called out his name she would flare up.

Because of her marrying Steven, her parents had disowned her and told her they had no daughter. They planned for her to attend college, but her agenda was different. Her parents hadn't spoken to her once in a seven year period. Her two brothers were in high school, and they would sneak by to visit her. She had a couple of aunts, uncles, and cousins who lived nearby, but she didn't have a relationship with them. She had no friends. It was just her and her kids.

She turned over as she thought about the day before—she had arrived home late, and everyday she was getting home later and later from work. Something was happening. Every morning for the past month when Vanessa arrived, she recognized an increase in her workload, whereas the other employees had the normal amount of work to do. But she couldn't track who was taking the mischievous actions against her. At times, the work was overwhelming.

She had started working at Graphs Unlimited as an office assistant one year ago. Margarita Williams was her supervisor, and she disapproved of Vanessa because she had three children with no father in their lives. She tried everything in her power to make Vanessa's days miserable. Vanessa didn't understand why Margarita detested her since she was the ideal employee. She was always on time, didn't take off from work much, and her work production was excellent. Regardless of what she was going through with her husband or the kids as a single parent, her financial situation, or Margarita's attitude, she remained positive towards her co-workers and the customers. Her conduct never changed with the everyday monotonous work routine.

As she reflected, it was a norm for her to entertain Margarita's presence at least twice in one day, but four times was excessive. Today, Margarita had come by her desk a fifth time, grinned crookedly and said, "Meet me in my office after your lunch." Vanessa had the sensation this meeting had nothing to do with her birthday. She smelled a dead rat in the atmosphere. And it was horrid enough to bring an adult man down to his knees.

Vanessa pondered the firing scenario when she had gone to Margarita's office as directed and saw her sitting at her cluttered desk fidgeting with an ink pen. Margarita faked a kind personality as she said, "Have a seat, Vanessa." She continued the conversation. "I have tried to be patient with you, but it seems that you can't seem to get your act together. This is the fifth time today that I've called you in my office. What is your problem? Your co-workers are complaining that they have to pull your workload." Margarita was an Afro-American woman, tall, medium framed, with short hair and glasses, and she dressed in a sophisticated way. She talked unprofessionally, was vicious, and had turned all her employees against Vanessa. "I have warned you that company policy states if an employee isn't productive and is reprimanded more than four times in one day, that's grounds to fire them on the spot. As you know, this is your fifth time in the office." Looking Vanessa straight in the eyes with a curt smile, she raised her tone and said, "Vanessa you're fired! There's a police officer outside the door to escort you off the premises."

Vanessa remembered her moment of joy when she started clapping her hands loud, trying to be strong although she felt weak. She didn't want Margarita to see her brokenness so she said, "Bravo! Bravo! It was you that set me up."

At that time, the police officer ran into the office and stood inside the door. "Is everything all right?" he asked. And Margarita nodded her head. Still in her strength with a meek tone she continued, "Margarita, you've done everything in your power to destroy me for the past months, so today is your lucky day." She remembered clapping louder and louder as she said, "You have succeeded and your strategy was clever. I needed this job because I have three little mouths to feed, but I refuse to beg you. I won't fight to stay... "

Margarita interrupted her and said, "You can't stay. You're out of here this day, right now, go from my sight."

The police officer said, "Let's go, miss!"

Her head was pounding as she glanced over, lightheaded, at the clock and it displayed 5:45 P.M. She must have fallen asleep. She jumped up, moaned, and held her head from the excruciating pain she was experiencing. The latest pickup time for the daycare was six o'clock. She needed time to come up with a plan. Vanessa remembered that Jasmine had a friend at the daycare, and her mother had offered assistance if she was ever late. "What's the girl's name? She remembered the little girl's name, but not her mother's. She went searching for the business card that had been given to her the previous day by the strange woman." As Vanessa held one side of her face with one hand, she remembered the card was on the refrigerator. "Taffi, that's her name."

She called the number on the card. "Taffi James," she said and continued, "I'm Jasmine's mother. We met yesterday at the daycare, and you offered to help if I was ever late. I took your card never considering that I would have to call you, but I'm desperate. Do you mind picking up all three of my children today because I need to…"

Taffi interrupted, "You don't have to explain a thing. I'll pick them up."

"Will you take them to your place? And I'll pick them up later. I have your address and know the street that you live on," Vanessa added.

Chapter 2

Five years had passed since Taffi had given birth to Esther who was a kindergarten student at Pine Outreach Academy. Time had moved fast. Taffi still wanted to fulfill her destiny now that she had turned thirty-one-years old. Moving forward was all she wanted to do because more was ahead. After all that she had gone through during the past years, she had matured beyond her age. She had never imagined that she would stay with her parents as long as she had since Esther's birth, but she loved being in their presence. It was convenient, and it stopped the loneliness she felt. They had been a blessing in her and Esther's lives. Deep down, though, she felt she might hinder her destiny if she continued living with her parents.

She had procrastinated taking the next step toward her destiny in fear of hurting her parents. She had called life a rural road adventure one-month prior when she went on a one-day excursion to a private country clubhouse in Colonial County, Virginia. The clubhouse specialized in providing a day of pampering with massages, facials, pedicures, and full body makeovers. On this adventure, she rolled down her car windows and let the wind blow through her hair as she headed toward her destination.

She traveled unpaved dirt roads that sometimes went uphill and, at times, had sharp curves. She had come across some roads without signs and had gone the wrong direction several times. No traffic lights existed to direct the traffic, and movement was risky. Trees covered both sides of the road, adding height as giants. Because of the integrated bushes and tall crops that sometimes grew close to the roads, visibility was limited. A couple of times, she witnessed deer leaping into the rural road. The more she drove, the more it reminded her of her life—at times, it was smooth, and sometimes it was rough. She was at the point in her life when she needed to make a sound decision about her destiny. Life had its ups and down. Even though leaving her parents to be out on her own was going to be a downhill drive at first, setting out to fulfill her destiny was going to be an uphill climb.

After the rural road adventure, when she walked inside her parents house, she over heard her mom say to Esther, "Grandpa and grandma could never live without you, baby doll." That night after much consideration, Taffi decided to call her realtor, and she purchased a home the next day.

When Kate and Paul Thomas heard the news of them leaving, they cried for weeks as though they were moving a million miles away. They wanted them to stay right where they were, although they knew that Taffi was old enough to venture out on her own. It was an emotional move, and no one wanted it to ensue. Despite emotions, Taffi was motivated and ready to start anew.

Taffi was now the director of Teen House, and she retained her position as the Network Engineer for the Pine Outreach Center. Her promotion to director was gratifying because helping and encouraging teens to keep their babies instead of giving them up by way of adoption or abortion was spectacular. She loved the teens despite their situations. The Teen House also offered classes to all patrons who needed to learn basic clerical and computer skills. She recognized that her destiny was to help and love others.

Pine Outreach Center had undergone major renovations, including the addition of the daycare and the Academy, which housed the first through sixth graders. When Kate became the Director of the Pine Outreach Academy and the daycare, the enrollments skyrocketed to full capacity. The primary function of the daycare was to provide reasonable service to disadvantaged customers so they wouldn't have to remain jobless because of unaffordable childcare costs. Kate chose customers with two or more kids and provided the care for little of nothing, as long as the moms showed they had continual legitimate employment. The system allowed women who wanted to work the chance to bring their children into a Christian environment. In addition, if they didn't have a church home, the Academy offered them a place to worship.

Taffi got her new house decorated and furnished. They had lived in it for two weeks when Taffi went to the daycare to pick up Esther and noticed a woman handling two small children. At first, she waved at her and walked over to speak to the woman. The woman had stopped at the same daycare class that Esther was attending. When Taffi looked in the classroom, she noticed that Esther and a blond haired girl were playing peacefully together. They were the only two kids in the room. As the two adults waited at the door for their children, Taffi felt it was an opportune time to offer free babysitting to her, in case she ever missed the pickup time or needed a break. She offered the woman her services because she saw how late the woman was in picking up her children. She had never met the woman before but she handed her a business card with her number on it anyway. Taffi felt something special about this woman and sensed that destiny would reveal the answers to the mystery, and soon.

She was shocked when she heard from Vanessa the next day. Her heart had gone out to this woman, and there was no way she was going to disappoint her when she needed her. Taffi picked up Vanessa's children without hesitation. But she hadn't understood why the day before she felt impelled to give the strange woman her card. She knew now it was to help her out. She even wondered if this was her destiny.

When Taffi looked at her clock, it displayed almost 8 P.M., and Vanessa hadn't picked up her kids. Taffi did the Christian thing and fed them dinner. At ten o'clock, Vanessa still hadn't called or shown up. She put the kids down for bed in her spare rooms. She went into the living room to wait for Vanessa's arrival, and at 11 P.M., she was still waiting. Taffi checked her caller I.D., but the number wasn't available. She said, "I hope everything is all right with Vanessa."

Taffi fell asleep on the sofa waiting for Vanessa. At midnight, she went to the bathroom after checking on the kids. When she returned to the sofa, she heard a faint tap on the door. Opening the door, she was face-to-face with Vanessa who looked drained of life and flushed with her hair mangled. As she entered, she wiped her nose with a tissue, and tears cropped up faster than she wiped them off. "Come in, Vanessa, and tell me what's going on with you," Taffi said, swallowing hard and escorting what was left of a crushed woman into her house. "Vanessa?" she questioned.

"I'm in a mess, and I have nowhere to turn," Vanessa admitted. "Never in my lifetime would I imagine my life to turn out as it has now. I'm going in a downward spiral with no way of coming out. This morning I was thinking how I loved the sunrise. But the sun set on my life right before my eyes, and there's not enough sunlight to make things all right," she cried. Taffi began to pat her on the back. Vanessa waited before she continued, "I would've given up, had it not been for my wonderful children. They were cold ice cream bars on a blazing hot summer day to me. I don't want to lose them or to let them see me in this state. Thank you so much for picking them up."

Taffi replied, "I didn't mind, because they were well behaved kids."

Vanessa cried again, but this time with her head hung low in shame, as she spoke, "I was fired yesterday by my wicked supervisor. She had set me up for the fall. And to top it off, when I got home from work, I found an eviction notice posted on my door. My husband…well, he's another nightmare along with my family. I have no place to go. After work, I'm so busy with the children that I have no friends. I called my property owner at her home to get her to change her decision about evicting me, but she said no because my apartment is already rented out the day after I vacate the premises. I'm a victim of horrible circumstances and right now, I don't know what to do. What a wonderful birthday present I received, huh?"

Taffi reached for a tissue to give Vanessa and said, "I believe everything people go through has a meaning. Trials and tribulations give you a testimony and make you a stronger person. The key is to live and not die through your hard times, humiliations, toils and sufferings. Satan is a liar when he says it's over. It's not!

"Right now, you perhaps can't see beyond your problems, and you think your life is over. I'm here to tell you that I was on a rural road adventure six years ago when my husband passed after Esther's conception. I thought the sharp curves would overtake me. Afterward my mom almost died, and I suffered a severe case of postpartum depression. That wasn't enough because after that Esther got sick and had to have emergency surgery. Over is not the word. I thought I would never see the sunrise again. But God made a way out of no way and delivered me.

"Hang in there because God will see you through this turmoil. There's a reason our paths met. I have a suggestion for you. I work at the Teen House, a place for pregnant teens to live when they have no other place to go. Tomorrow, I was to hire a new residential manager, but instead, I'll give the job to you. You can stay in a two-bedroom apartment there until you're able to get back on your feet. For the rest of the week, you can stay here while you move your things out of your apartment."

Vanessa's tear-drained eyes focused on Taffi with delight, as a child receiving a lollipop. "Your suggestion is a blessing, but I have one question to ask, thank you. Why are you helping me out?" she asked.

"What are friends for, but to help and show love to one another? One day, maybe you'll return the same favor to someone else in need. Tomorrow morning, once you get yourself together after resting, you go get your kids some clean clothes from your apartment. Let them spend the night here. Don't disturb them now, they need their beauty sleep," Taffi said.

Vanessa looked at her with rising joy, "Taffi, I…I …."

Taffi interrupted by putting her finger to her mouth, "Don't say another word. I have an empty room in the back or you're welcomed to sleep on the sofa whichever you prefer."

"I'll be right back. I think it'll be better if I go and get our clothes now," Vanessa answered smiling, contented that her situation was resolved.

"Vanessa I'll feel much better if you'll wait until tomorrow morning since it is late outside for an unaccompanied female."

"Don't worry, I'll be all right. I have my car. I'll run in and out within minutes. It's still early," Vanessa glimpsed down at her watch and ignored her concerns. "It's one in the morning, the night is early. Moreover, the sun has risen in my life, and the darkness is fading away. I'm all right. What could happen now that the worst is over?"

Chapter 3

Vanessa's neighbor from across the hall awakened at three in the morning because of her loud television. It was apparent that she had rolled over on the remote control. As she turned it down, she thought she heard groaning from outside the door. She heard the sound again and decided to explore through her peephole. She saw nothing. She thought maybe it was an injured animal, but when she opened the door, she was alarmed to see her neighbor knocked out by her door. Blood was everywhere even on the cement walls. She was horizontal, stretched out on the cement floor face up. The neighbor asked, "Are you all right," But Vanessa wasn't responding. She rushed and called the paramedics and the police. When the paramedics got there, Vanessa had stopped breathing. The paramedics worked hard to revive her.

Sgt. Perry was the officer on duty who responded to the call. He noticed that the injured female was the same woman he had escorted out of Graphs Unlimited the day before. Her condition stabilized enough for them to transport her to the hospital. He questioned the neighbor, but she didn't know any information about what had happened to Vanessa. She knew her first name was Vanessa and didn't know what had happened to her or anything about her family. He rummaged around Vanessa's purse to find out more information about her. He found a business card of an honorable person in the community who he happened to know from his college days. They had attended Pine University together and graduated nine years ago.

He called the number on the business card, and Taffi recognized his voice before he even stated his name. They chatted about what they had done with their lives since graduation. He told her that he joined the police force, lived in his own home, and he had had women falling at his feet, being a single man.

She told him about when she met her husband Donald, how he had died and left her to rear Esther alone.

He said, "You may not remember, but the day your husband died, I was one of the officers at the scene. You were hysterical. You may have not seen me. I'm sorry about your husband and your mother."

"Mother's fine. She lived."

"Good! He said.

After they finished the personal conversation, Sgt. Perry got down to business and asked, "Do you know a woman by the name of Vanessa? Is she a relative?"

Taffi told him about Vanessa's unfortunate hardships and how she had left a couple of hours ago to pick up some clothing for her kids and herself and was coming right back to her house, but hadn't returned yet. "I was getting worried," she said. "Her kids are staying at my house now. Is she in any trouble?"

He told her about the severe trauma to her head and that she was in intensive care at Pine Hospital.

"Will I be able to visit her? Was she beat up? Is she alive?" Taffi asked.

"There's a waiting room, but she's in intensive care where visitation is limited to immediate family members. Right now, it is too early to determine her fate. When the ambulance left her residence, she was still alive. Until we question her, we don't know what happened to her because no witnesses have come forth yet. Do you know her family or the name of her husband, since she has children?" he asked.

"Sgt. Perry, I've been acquainted with Vanessa on a personal basis for a short time. She had my business card and called me to pick up her kids from daycare. She spoke about her wicked supervisor who fired her on yesterday, her eviction notice, her deadbeat husband, and her terrible family that has shunned her. I hope that'll help you out some. I'm sorry this had to happen to her." Taffi said.

"It sounds as though she had a lot on her plate. I hope that we'll find the underlying cause of this. Thank you for your help," he said, as he hung up the telephone.

Taffi called Kate to come stay with the kids while she went to the hospital. She was the only person in the waiting room until Sgt. Perry strolled into the room, and she recognized him right off because he hadn't changed one bit. He came across as a firm officer, but was gentle as a kitten, and his childish grin gave him away. His medium frame, along with his six-foot stature, made him look good in uniform. His eyes were equal to looking into the blue sky on a sunny day. He had blonde hair, was Caucasian and a handsome fellow.

She tried to see Vanessa, but as Sgt. Perry stated, only immediate family could visit. He had rushed his investigation and found her immediate family members within an hour, so her mother and her father were there. Sgt. Perry attempted to get in touch with Steven, her husband, with no luck.

Vanessa's parents didn't speak to Taffi or to Sgt. Perry. Within five minutes of their arrival, the doctor came into the waiting area and asked for her husband or parents. The standoffish couple walked over to him. Sgt. Perry whispered to Taffi, "That's her parents, Earl and Jennifer Moore."

Vanessa's mom looked to be in her late forties and was a redhead. She perhaps was once an attractive woman, but her age showed. She had a medium figure and looked to be about five and a half feet tall, and she smelled of cigarettes. She was a puppet to her husband, and he guarded her every move.

Her father was every bit of six feet tall, if not more. He had a thickset build with a beer belly, wore glasses, and was neat in his casual clothing. He was clean-cut with brown eyes and hair. He held his mouth to one side as he chewed on beef jerky. He didn't look to be someone to reckon with easily.

Taffi and Sgt. Perry listened as the doctor explained her status. "Vanessa's head injuries are severe, and she's in and out of consciousness. There's the possibility that she won't make it through the day." After they heard the news, her father took her mother by the hand and said, "Let's go," and they rushed away. Taffi found it strange that they would run off after learning of her severe condition.

Vanessa made it through the first day and night, still in critical condition, in and out of consciousness. Everyday Taffi went home to change her clothing and returned to the waiting room, hoping for a change in Vanessa's status. At five in the morning on the third day of hospitalization, Vanessa's condition changed for the better. She was conscious and requested that Taffi visit her, and they allowed her into the room. Vanessa had refused the feeding tubes or medications once she regained consciousness. Vanessa's parents hadn't shown up since the first short visit. Taffi felt lucky that she had a wonderful relationship with her parents and that they were there for her no matter what. Before she went into Vanessa's room, she called Kate to let her know that she would be home later because Vanessa was conscious.

Taffi entered the room and envisioned seeing the same healthy woman she had encountered days before. Instead, she saw a pale colored woman dressed in a blue cotton hospital gown with black and blue marks on her face, arms, and legs. As she lay in the bed, her body was almost lifeless. Her eyes told the story of her hard life, the struggles, and the pains she encountered.

Taffi went and sat near Vanessa's bed and took hold of her hand, and tears were flowing down her face. Vanessa managed to whisper, "I've known you a short time, but I want you to have full custody of my children if anything should happen to me. Could you handle the responsibility of bringing up three young children plus the one of your own?"

Taffi replied, "Stop talking as if something negative is going to happen to you. God is able to bring you out of this ordeal. Think positive because your life is not over." Taffi grinned, but Vanessa was serious.

Vanessa was quick to point out, "The last couple of days, many angels have visited me . . . Once I handle my business, I'll be ready to go because I'm tired."

Taffi blushed in amazement. "Are you sure there's no one else to mother your children?" she asked.

Vanessa dropped her eyes as she turned away from Taffi. "No, I want you to care for them. Remember, you said there a reason our paths met. Well, I believe your destiny is to raise my children."

Taffi nodded, "I remember the conversation."

Vanessa swallowed hard, "Well, I know now that it wasn't meant for me to stay, but for my children to stay with you."

"Are you sure? Maybe the anesthesia and medications you're taking are making you talk impractically," Taffi said, trying to reason with Vanessa.

"I'm not being impractical," Vanessa retorted. "I know my time is up, and I don't want to go on anymore," she said, as tears started to flow from her eyes.

Taffi reached for a tissue on the nightstand and wiped Vanessa's tears. "If you feel that I'm the person, so be it, but why me?" she asked.

"You're sincere, true, caring and genuine; therefore, why not you, Taffi? I liked you the first time I met you. Your qualities seem great. Perhaps I'm doing what your husband did when he left you after you conceived Esther, but please don't get mad. In addition, I don't want Steven to ever get my children, never Taffi, unless he changes, which I feel will never happen," Vanessa gawked at Taffi. "Nor do I want my parents to have them either, if they ever would want them," she said. "Nor do I want his family to have them. If any of them try to fight because you're no kin to us, stand firm because they'll never love my children as you. I believe that truth in my heart, despite the short time we've been together. Your heart is real."

Taffi pointed out, "Vanessa, there's a story in the Bible, that's found in Luke 14: 1-6, that I'll enlighten you about before I answer your question. I just read this yesterday. I guess its confirmation on what I should do. It was a Sabbath, and a chief Pharisee gave a supper as they watched Jesus. God commanded there be no work on the Sabbath. It is a rest day. In front of Jesus was a man with Dropsy, a disease that causes excessive water in the tissue. Jesus asked if it was lawful to heal on the Sabbath. The Pharisees remained silent. If they said 'yes,' they couldn't condemn Jesus for healing. Saying 'No,' would condemn them for being uncaring to human suffering. Jesus healed the man and sent him away. Jesus asked them, 'If one of you had a son or an ox that falls into a well on the Sabbath, would you not pull him out?' They remained silent and didn't answer Him. Vanessa, will I pull you out of the well? Providing supportive acts or helping someone whenever necessary is my duty. My answer to you is yes, I promise to take good care of your children," Taffi squeezed Vanessa's hand firm to reassure her of the promise she'd made.

With tears in her eyes, Vanessa moaned from the pain she was feeling and said, "Thank you," and she fell asleep.

Two hours later, when Vanessa awakened, Sgt. Perry took her statement as to what happened the night she was injured. Vanessa glared at him and, still speaking in her soft tone, she murmured, "I left home at around 8:00 P.M. that night to pick up my kids from Taffi's house. As I drove, I knew that it was too early to face anyone in the condition I was in, so I parked my car in a deserted parking lot and waited until I was composed enough to talk to Taffi in person. I had lost my job, as you know, since you're the officer who escorted me out of my office. I also received an eviction notice the same day."

She smiled and continued, "But I found a true friend in Taffi who was willing to help me out." She winked at Taffi. "I returned home at about 1:15 A.M. to get clothing for my children and myself, since we would be staying with Taffi." She tried to raise her head but the movement took all her energy away.

"I got out of my car. I dropped my keys and leaned down to pick them up. After I picked them up, I headed toward my apartment. As I walked, I noticed Steven getting out of a brand new black truck. He must have remembered that it was my birthday. The last time he departed eighteen months ago, I made double sure that he wouldn't get into my apartment. I had all the locks changed, and I never gave him a spare key.

"He jumped out staggering, furious, asking, 'Where have you been and where are my children?' He met me on the sidewalk. I smelled alcohol on his breath. He shouted, 'You've been out messing around all night long, haven't you?' He didn't know I was going through tragedy in my life and didn't care about my problems. I was infuriated after seeing the truck. I told him he had no right to tell me what I should or shouldn't do and, if he wanted me to be at home, then he should be there paying the bills and taking care of the male responsibilities. Instead, he was out buying new trucks and living a single lifestyle. For the past four months, I have begged him for help, to pay my bills, to buy the kid's clothes, to be there for them, but all I get is $5 or $10 after his late night visits when the kids are asleep. I told him that wasn't enough, and I didn't have to take it anymore. And since he refused to be a father or a husband, he had no right to stand there asking me where I've been. I said, 'It's none of your business where I've been or who I've been out with. The day you take responsibility is the day you'll have authority over my children or me, but until then, get lost.' I slapped his face, turned away from him. He pulled my arm, but I shook loose and continued heading for my apartment. Staggering because of his drunken stupor, he followed me a short way as he grabbed my arm again saying, 'No wife of mine will ever talk to me that way.' He looked at me. I've never witnessed an appearance as devilish as his. I yanked loose from his grip and ran toward my apartment building. I heard him say, 'Go, I don't want you anyway, and if money's an issue, huh! You keep the $5, he said as he sped off in his truck."

Vanessa body turned to ice as she talked, "After opening the main entrance door, the narrow heel of my shoe got stuck in a large crack. My foot turned over, my shoe flew off, I tripped, and my head hit the hard cement wall. The door slammed against my foot. At that point, I was still conscious, but in lots of pain. I tried to pull my body up and open the door to release the pressure off my jammed foot. I dragged my foot inside the building and fell against the cement wall. I headed toward my neighbor's door for help because I knew no one was at my apartment. I was in pain, and her television was loud. I knew she didn't hear me fall or my shouts for help. I hit my head countless times trying to free myself from the door. I remembered my neighbor coming outside and that's all." Sgt. Perry turned his crimson colored face away.

Taffi was sitting near Vanessa's bedside as she told the story.

After Sgt. Perry left, Vanessa said, "I feel tired."

Taffi responded, "You've been through a lot. I'll step out and let you rest.

Vanessa said, "No, you don't understand. I'm tired. Tell my children that I love them and that I was a good mother. At my apartment, you'll find pictures and a journal with an account of their entire upbringing. Let them come to my funeral, but don't let them see me dying. It may scare them. Talk about me to them often and show them my pictures," she demanded.

"Hurry, I need you to get me a lawyer to write me a last will and testament. Time is ending for me. Also, my insurance policies are active for one-month past my discharge date from my job. That'll help you out financially, but hurry." Vanessa's voice started to trail off and her breathing became heavier. Every inch of her body was weakening with every breath she took. She moaned from the pain that she was experiencing, but she never complained.

Taffi ran to the phone and called Aaron Kin, her lawyer, and she called her father to come right over. Aaron entered the room in a three-piece navy suit. He was a young, professional fellow with strong knowledge of the law. He had his own firm and loved to be available when needed. He came right over with a "Do Not Resuscitate Order" for Vanessa to sign and the "Last Will and Testament." Vanessa explained to Aaron how Steven had avoided his parental obligations, and she stressed her desire for him not to gain custody of her children. Aaron advised her to let Taffi be a standby guardian if she became unable to care for her children or in the event of her death.

After Aaron pointed out her options, Paul Thomas entered the room and introduced himself, "Taffi has told me good things about you. I'm her father, Pastor Thomas. I'm glad to meet you."

"Hi, sir, I'm glad to meet you," Vanessa said. She studied Paul Thomas before continuing, "I have asked your daughter to be the guardian over my children, and she has agreed. I feel in my heart that they are getting the best and meeting you affirm in my heart that I've made the correct decision." She continued but with forceful breathing, "I have designated Taffi as a standby guardian to become the sole guardian if I die before the commencement of judicial proceeding to appoint her as guardian of my minor children." Paul Thomas and Aaron witnessed Vanessa's written acceptance of relinquishing her guardianship to Taffi.

Once she duly executed the will, Aaron Kin left the room. Uneasy Vanessa said, "I feel tired."

"Vanessa, God loves you so much that He sent His only Son as an atoning sacrifice for your sins. Jesus knew this time in your life would come. He can take away every tear from your eyes and give you the desires of your heart. He's the beginning and the end. All you have to do is ask. Don't you want to be healed?"

"Pastor Thomas," she paused and took a deep breath. "No sir, I," she took another breath, "don't want to be healed," as her voice started to fade. "I'm tired," she took another breath. "I feel my time," she paused, "on earth is finished." She continued at almost a whisper, "I want," she took a deep breath, "to know Jesus," and then another breath, "before I go." She was motionless on the bed.

She listened with her eyes shut as Paul Thomas spoke, "Vanessa, salvation is easy because all you have to do is repent for being a sinner and confess with your mouth that Jesus Christ is Lord. Acknowledge that He died on the cross and believe in your heart that He rose on the third day. I'll sprinkle you with some water, and you'll know Him." She confessed her sins and accepted Christ as her Savior between breaths.

Sgt. Perry visited Vanessa after two that afternoon and updated her on the investigation, "We have your husband in custody at the city jail. We found him in Ohio yesterday. "

Following Sgt. Perry's report, Vanessa's health deteriorated, and she started to breathe louder and louder. Vanessa looked up at Taffi, smiled, and said in her normal clear voice without the hard breathing, "I should have known Him sooner. He is waiting for me. I have to go." She motioned for Taffi to hold her hand, smiled at her as she said, "Will you promise to tell my kids that I love them, and tell Steven that I forgive him?" Her face had gone rigid, her eyes went blank, as she took her last breath.

Paul Thomas hugged Taffi as she began to cry, "Yes, I promise Vanessa, yes," she blurted out crying. Sgt. Perry had stepped outside the room, but when he heard the crying, he returned. Both Paul Thomas and Sgt. Perry started comforting Taffi.

The death scene had rekindled old flames in her memory. She recognized the negative thinking and she shook it off as she clinched Paul Thomas and Sgt. Perry's hands.

They held her hands tightly, and then Paul Thomas released his hand from hers and pulled the sheet over the dead body before calling for the nursing staff. Paul Thomas said, "Vanessa's chapter in life has ended, but, Taffi, yours is beginning as the mother of four children."

Life had changed swiftly before her eyes. She dared not fathom where this road was taking her. She felt that, if God was directing her, everything was going to be all right.

Her life was on another rural road adventure. Maybe this time the journey would take her to her destiny. She looked at her father, "I have a favor to ask you, dad. Will you go home with me and help me break the news to Vanessa's kids? You have more experience at doing this than I." Paul Thomas followed her home and Sgt. Perry, who was still on duty, went with them.

Chapter 4

Taffi rode in the car wordlessly with her father as she thought about her new chapter in life. She knew that she had promised Vanessa something big, but now it was all coming to light. The first undertaking wasn't going to be pleasurable, but heartrending. To tell three children that they'd never be with their mother again was horrendous. She had to be strong because her task was hard. Explaining the death of a mother to small children was more than she wanted to bear.

Vanessa had requested that she take care of her funeral arrangements. Vanessa's parents were out the picture. Taffi wondered why animosity had come between them. And why on her deathbed they couldn't forgive and let it go. They let a stranger take care of her children instead of them stepping up to the plate. Taffi remembered when Vanessa asked her if anyone had stopped by, and, when she told her that her parents visited for a short time once, Vanessa had squeezed her eyes tightly shut. Taffi knew that she was disappointed. Taffi couldn't even imagine her parents not stepping up to the plate and taking on their grandparental responsibilities. She stared at her father because of the love and respect she had for him. He was wise, strong, wonderful man, and she needed his support more than ever.

When they arrived, Kate was in the kitchen preparing snacks for the children. She was a good mother figure, and her love for children and her ability to be attentive to their needs was astonishing. She had taken a week off to help Taffi with the children. Instead of taking them to the daycare, she resumed the role of mother and stayed home with them, loved, nurtured and fed them. Taffi loved her mom's ability to love. When Taffi had been in a rut and didn't take care of her responsibilities as a mother, Kate had stepped in and did it for her until she was strong. Taffi motioned to Kate with her lips that they needed to talk. Taffi took her aside and told her that Vanessa had passed. Kate suggested that they reveal the news in the living room after the kids ate, for it wouldn't spoil their little appetites. Paul Thomas, Sgt. Perry, and Taffi went ahead to the living room and held polite conversation while they waited for them.

After about ten minutes, Kate escorted the three older kids in the room and took the baby away to change him. The kids were smiling and talking about which cartoons they were going to watch on television. Taffi interrupted them and said, "Why don't you'll come over here? I have to talk to you about something important before you watch the television."

They took a seat on the floor and watched her mouth as she began. "Jasmine and Jackie, I have a question to ask, would you want to stay in my house with Esther and me to live?"

Jasmine answered her with yes and Jackie said yes. Jasmine picking her nose asked, "Will my mom and brother get to stay here too?"

Taffi closed her eyes as Paul Thomas rescued her by saying, "I sure would love for you to stay here." He smiled as the children turned and looked at him.

Taffi continued, "I talked to your mom in the hospital, and she wanted you Jasmine, Jackie, and Eric, all three of you, to stay here." She blew out a breath, "Do any of you know what dying is?"

Esther raised her hand, but spoke out before anyone answered, "Yes, I do mommy."

"What is dying sweetheart?" Taffi repeated.

"Grandpa said," and she glanced at Paul Thomas and he winked back at her, "it's when people get tired, fall asleep on this earth, and never wake up when they sleep. They go up to heaven, wake up there, and live with God forever, if they are good, or go down there," she pointed her finger toward the floor, "if they are bad. He said, 'It is something that every person will do,'" Esther threw an appreciative look at him and he understood.

"Jasmine and Jackie, do you understand what Esther said?" Taffi asked. Jasmine nodded, but Jackie looked puzzled. Jasmine said, "Yes, we have seen it on television, and our mommy explained it to us before. She told us that her mom and father had died right after she got married."

Taffi looked suspicious because she knew why her parents didn't stay at the hospital, because of old issues stemming from her marriage.

"Jasmine and Jackie, I went everyday to see your mother in the hospital. She loved you all. I have something to tell you," she said and motioned to them, "Come here, please." They stood and Jackie jumped on Taffi' lap while Jasmine sat close by her side and she hugged her tight. "What I'm going to say hurts, and it's all right if you cry. Your mom is now sleeping in heaven," Taffi said, without hesitation, although she wanted to cry. She felt she had to be straightforward and strong.

Jasmine understood and started to cry, but Jackie didn't understand. She looked around, confused as to why her sister was crying.

"Will I see my mommy when she wakes up?" Jasmine asked all of a sudden after she played with the lace on her dress.

Taffi answered her, "If you go to heaven, you'll see her again."

Jasmine started to cry and throw bogus punches in the air. She yelled, "I want my mommy. I want my mommy."

Jackie started to yell, "I want my mommy."

Paul Thomas interjected, "Jasmine, its okay to be sad when someone you love dies and goes away. Did you know that Jesus was sad sometimes? "

Jasmine calmed down and Taffi interjected, "Jasmine, I was sad when Esther's father died over five years ago. I cried and cried because I loved him. It's okay to cry. One day, God helped me to be happy again. Your mom is not alone because Esther's father, Donald, is there along with my Great-Grandma Campbell. You, Jackie, and Eric aren't alone either because you have all of us." Taffi pointed her finger toward all the people in the room. "Whenever you want to talk about your feelings, come to me. I'm going to give you a notebook to write or draw what you're feeling."

Jasmine confirmed by giving Taffi a gigantic hug, "okay." Taffi entrusted each one with a notebook and colored pencils.

The adults went into the kitchen, and the kids remained in the living room watching television. Sgt. Perry said, "That went perfectly, and I think they understood what happened to their mother.

"I agree," said Taffi as she nodded along with Paul Thomas.

"The interpretation of dying, coming from a child's perspective made clarification easier," Paul Thomas admitted. "And I thought Esther wasn't listening to me that closely last year."

The next day Taffi and Sgt. Perry went over to Vanessa's apartment and sorted through her belongings. She decided to take the children's bedroom furniture and toys in order that they would feel some connection to home. She found the journal, pictures, and an address book. The rest of the things in the house they took to a local thrift shop.

The following day was the viewing at the funeral home, and Taffi had put a wonderful eulogy in the *Pine Crest Newspaper*. Paul Thomas had agreed to have the home going service at his church on the morning after the viewing.

Taffi had decided to take the kids to the viewing. When they drove up to the funeral home, numerous cars were out front and young adults were outside the building. As Taffi got out of the car, she said to Kate, "There sure are a lot of people here for the viewing." They inched their way through the crowd in the corridor and entered the first room they saw. It was full of people, but when they looked at the body, it wasn't Vanessa's body. Instead, it was a young man in the casket. They backtracked and entered a conjoining room where the atmosphere was different. It was colder, quieter, and smaller. The flowers in the serene atmosphere, along with the bright clothing that Vanessa was wearing, brightened the room. The makeup had done wonders to her bruised body.

Paul Thomas drove the three older children to the viewing in order to discuss what they were going to see and to be a support to them. As he drove, he told Jasmine, "Sweetheart, we're going to see your mommy today. When you see her, she won't move. If you touch her, she will be hard and cold. And if you talk to her, she can't talk back to you because she is sleeping in heaven. You may feel sad, and it's all right for you to cry. When he stopped the car and unbuckled them, he gave each one a kiss and a big hug.

Jasmine entered the room with Paul Thomas, and when she saw her mother, she ran toward her crying aloud. "Mommy, we missed you." Jackie, not knowing what was happening, cried from Jasmine's reaction. Taffi picked up Jackie and comforted her. Esther sat between Taffi and Kate who was holding baby Eric. Paul Thomas had followed Jasmine, and when she reached the casket, she stood there and looked at her mother, bawling. They allowed her time about five minutes with her mother. She tugged on Paul Thomas's jacket, "Can I kiss her?" He lifted her up and she almost leaped out of his arms, but he grabbed her tight. She leaned over and gave her mom the biggest compassionate hug and kiss. Afterward she glanced at Paul Thomas and asked, "Why is she cold and hard?"

He said, "Sweetheart, when people die, that's how they feel." She looked at Vanessa a final time and said, "Good night, mommy." Paul Thomas took the kids home while Taffi and Kate stayed until the viewing period was over. No one showed up while they where there. As they departed the room, people gathered everywhere to visit the family of the young man in the next room. Kate went to the bathroom, and Taffi stayed in the corridor. She asked a group of young women what happened to the young man in the casket, and one of the young women told her that an accident had occurred when a gun went off and a stray bullet killed him right away.

When they got in the car, Taffi told Kate about the young man's cause of death. "Mom, I noticed that the obituary today had at least six people under the age of 26. This world is getting bad, and it's evident that the end of this world is near." She sighed, "Although Vanessa discovered the Lord on her deathbed, we at least know that she was saved and knew the Lord a short time before she left here. I hope those people had the opportunity to know God before they left here."

"To depart this world unsaved is horrible, but many people say they have time, because nothing will happen to them. They live life to the fullest, doing whatever pleases them, and wait until they get old to settle down and turn their lives over to Christ. They don't appreciate that tomorrow not promised to anyone. In minutes, a life can leave this world. God is awesome and those who don't know Him before leaving this world are missing an amazing Savior. I've never regretted serving the Lord," Kate said.

"Mom, I think some people think that they have to give up everything when they turn to God, but they don't realize that the things they are turning from are bad for them anyway." After verbalizing her thoughts, Taffi drove in silence thinking about Jasmine. When she picked up the children, they were playing as though everything was normal. She concluded that she was over-evaluating the situation for nothing because children bounce back quickly.

The next morning the home going ceremony for Vanessa was at Pine Outreach Center at 10 A.M. Taffi had decided to have a closed casket ceremony because she didn't want the children to suffer too much trauma. The night before, Jasmine had kept Taffi up whimpering throughout the night. Each time Taffi would pat her back, and she would stop crying and fall back to sleep.

When Taffi arrived at the ceremony, she was shocked that the church had a packed house for Vanessa's home going. After Taffi and the children sat down, two male teenagers came over and greeted Taffi. One teenager was wearing eyeglasses, a cashmere sweater and pressed slacks. He had light brown hair, and was distinguished looking. He said, "Hi, I'm Adam, Vanessa's younger brother, and this is Joseph our older brother." They all shook hands. "We've heard about the goodness you've shown toward our sister and wanted to thank you for what you've done for her and her children. We had to be here today, and we know it's worth any punishment that we'll receive. We used to sneak over to her house sometimes to visit against our parents commands. We loved our sister and had to say good-bye to her today."

Joseph was laid-back, dressed sportily, and was tall whereas Adam was short. His hair was blonde, the same color as Vanessa's. Both had southern accents. He said, "We love our sister. Thank you for supporting her during her hospitalization. I wish I were older, because I would take Vanessa's children. Can we keep in touch with them? That's the least we can do for her."

Taffi answered them with a hug, "Of course you can keep in touch. You're welcome at anytime. Come and sit where you should be sitting, next to your sister's children." Taffi felt inclined to start the service fifteen minutes later than scheduled. She followed her mind and was glad that she did because Earl and Jennifer Moore strolled up the aisle five minutes before the service was to start.

When Jennifer reached the casket she shouted, "Why is the casket closed?" Taffi turned to Kate as she walked toward them. People in the congregation had all eyes on them.

She said, "I want to see my daughter. Why is the casket closed?"

Taffi took her aside and said, "Mrs. Moore, I'm sorry about the casket being closed, but I'm looking out for the best interest of the children. Jasmine had nightmares last night. If you hang tight, I'll take the children out and allow you time with your daughter."

She calmed down after realizing what Taffi had said. "Okay," she said. Taffi took the kids out of the room to allow her time with her daughter.

Jennifer cried out as she hugged her daughter, "I'm sorry, Vanessa for the hatred I've shown you. I love you."

With tears in her eyes, she continued to lean over her daughter's body and cry. She hadn't slept in days, nor had she bathed or combed her hair. She was wearing a long-sleeved, flowered dress that came down below her knees. She smelled of cigarettes and alcohol. She was jittery and moved frequently. She was in disarray because she was stuck in the middle. She loved Vanessa, but she didn't want to frustrate Earl since he had shunned her.

She said, "Vanessa, I hope you will forgive me for turning my back on you." She cried for about ten minutes more, hugging her daughter's body.

As Jennifer spoke to her daughter, Earl walked over to her. He had no care in the world. He was uncomfortable in the environment. He smelled of alcohol. With a hateful stare he said, "Let's go, now! Enough of this hogwash! She's dead and gone, and that's the best place for her, the traitor."

She answered him, "No I'm staying." He staggered to the aisle opposite of where his sons sat. He pointed to them and loudly said, "You two are traitors too. Wait till you get home."

Jennifer took a seat on the same bench as her sons while Earl left the church. When the children re-entered, Paul Thomas started to preach from Joshua 16. "Joshua was old and had brought Israel to the blessings promised to them by Jacob and Moses. Israel was to conquer the Canaanite idol worshippers and receive their inheritance in Ephraim. They didn't drive them out, but instead they caused them to serve under tribute or taxation. Ephraim took the easy way out."

He continued, "Do you know that the easy way out is rarely the right way?" He asked, "Is there anybody here who has taken the easy way out? By not taking responsibility for your actions...Not doing what's right...Not committing to Christ...Has it ever haunted you?

"Vanessa didn't take the easy way out because she was able to confess Christ as her Savior on her dying bed. She decided to do the right thing. It will not come back to haunt her because she'll have eternal life. How about you? Have you made a commitment to Christ? To sin and to live how you want to is easy. Sex before marriage is easy. Doing drugs or alcohol to forget your hurts is the easy way out. To get a divorce instead of staying in a marriage and trying to make it work is the easy way out. Hanging around with the wrong people when you know they're bad influences is the easy way out. Buying on credit and getting in debt is the easy way out. Cheating instead of being honest is the easy way out. Stealing instead of working to purchase a product is the easy way out. Lying instead of being truthful is the easy way out. Hating instead of loving a person is the easy way out. Getting into a homosexual relationship because you feel unloved is the easy way out, instead of gaining a relationship with the lover of our souls, Jesus. Not forgiving instead of letting bygones be bygones is the easy way out. People, there's a way that is above all ways and that's to know the Lord Jesus as our personal Savior.

"Do you know Him as Savior? Vanessa knew Him and did what was right. I was in the hospital room before Vanessa passed, and she said, 'I should've known Him sooner.' People, the time wasn't too late for Vanessa because she was able to repent and confess that Jesus is Lord. But what if you got in an accident this morning and never regained consciousness? You would be lost forever. Do you want to discover freedom? The choice is yours. This is a funeral, but it's also a time for people to see the light and turn from the darkness.

"We have to come to Jesus right now because tomorrow isn't promised to us. Had Vanessa never regained consciousness, she would have never known Christ."

The music started to play and Paul Thomas waved the people to come to the altar, "Come to Jesus." Many people came to the altar, including Jennifer. It was an awesome home going ceremony because lives were changed.

Taffi had imagined that the adjustment period for the children would take a long time, but she was stunned when it turned out to be short. They had no problem adjusting.

The day after the funeral, Taffi was sitting in her bedroom reading a book on her chaise. She needed quality time to herself. About three months after Esther was born, she had started engaging in this relaxing activity at least three times per week. She used this time to pamper herself with reading fictional love stories. At about midnight, a piercing cry startled her. She ran to

Jasmine's nightlight lit room. When she entered, she saw that Jasmine was awake and frightened. Taffi ran to Jasmine's bed, as she pointed to the closet, tears flowing.

"What's wrong honey?" she questioned looking down at her.

She answered while pulling away and pointing at the closet, "I saw my mommy in the closet. Right there with my clothes."

Taffi went to the closet and turned on the light and said, "Look honey, there's no one in your closet."

"But I saw her," she insisted.

"Come here, Jasmine, and look for yourself."

"I saw her, Mrs. James." She studied the closet in silence.

Taffi watched her and assured her that nothing was in her closet. She held her hand securely as Jasmine kept peering at the dark. Taffi guided her to the bed, but Jasmine wailed, "No. No. I can't sleep in here. I'm scared."

"You can sleep in here because everything is all right. I'll be right back in here to get you if you need me, and you can sleep with the light on if you need to see."

"No, No," she screeched.

"Okay, follow me." Taffi and Jasmine went to the phone and called Paul Thomas. Taffi and Jasmine went into the living room to wait for him. Within a few minutes, he was there. They all sat on the sofa and Jasmine was sandwiched between Taffi and Paul Thomas. He said, "Jasmine, everything is all right." He held her hands together and patted them. "I believe you when you say you saw your mother in the closet."

"You do?" she asked, sounding surprised.

"Yes. If you say you saw her, I believe you." As he looked at her, she blew out an exasperated breath.

"Jasmine, your mother would never hurt you because she loved you and your brother and sister. She wanted to see you for her last time on earth before she goes to heaven," he said and hugged her. "I love you, and Taffi loves you, and your mother who's in heaven will always love you. You're a wonderful, loved little girl. Never hide what you're feeling. It's all right to cry, to laugh, to be sad, to be happy, or to think about your mom. I'm going to pick you up and take you to your room. Try not to be scared because I'm going to stay with you until you fall asleep. When we get in your room, I want you to be brave and tomorrow I want you to be even braver. She'll never hurt you."

He took her to her room and within minutes, she had fallen asleep.

Jasmine's nightmares stopped after about two weeks, but she continued to draw the pictures of her mother and her feelings. Two weeks after the nightmares stopped, Jasmine drew a colorful picture that touched Taffi. On the page, a woman was smack in the middle of the page. She was holding two girls in one hand, and a girl and little boy were in the other hand. In the right corner, was a picture of a woman looking down from heaven and waving at the woman and all the children. In the left top corner were two people flying side by side with wings. Taffi asked her to explain the picture, and Jasmine said, "This is a picture of my family. This is you Mommy J," she said and pointed to Taffi. "This is my mom in heaven," pointing to the woman waving. She managed a smile and said, "This is Esther and Jackie, plus me and my baby brother."

Taffi asked, "Who are the flying people?" and Jasmine shouted, "Silly, they're Grandma and Grandpa Thomas. Do you know they watch over us kids all the time?"

Taffi pinched her cheek and said, "Yes, they do watch over you kids all the time, and they even watch over me, too."

Jasmine said, "Wow! Gosh, you are a grownup!"

Before Taffi answered, Jasmine had run off to play with Esther.

Taffi looked at having four children as gratifying and not as an obligation to help Vanessa. The task was different, but Taffi was determined to be a bona fide survivor, since this was her destiny.

Chapter 5

One successful month had passed, and Taffi was optimistic that the new living arrangement would work out. Esther got along well with all the children, and they with her, and all were adjusting to the new living arrangements. The children had their own bedrooms. Sgt. Perry had transported all the furniture over the day after Vanessa died, but this weekend they were doing renovation, painting the walls and decorating each room per kid's choice to allow identities to surface. Taffi had asked each of the older children what characters they wanted in their rooms and went out and purchased bedspreads, curtains, and matching accessories.

Sgt. Perry was still coming around to help with the children. He even started to attend the church services and loved Paul Thomas's preaching. He and Taffi were becoming the best of friends. He was single and was always around. Taffi was single, but she saw him as a good friend and nothing more. He loved the children so much that he'd stop at yard sales and purchased all kinds of toys for them. Sometimes, he would even get on the floor and play with them. Before long, they'd grown attached to him.

Paul Thomas and Kate loved the fact they had four grandchildren instead of one grandchild. Although Taffi didn't give birth to them, they loved them all the same and treated them equally. They, along with Sgt. Perry, were going over to Taffi's at nine o'clock in the morning to help paint. Kate, Paul Thomas, Sgt. Perry, and Taffi gathered to paint.

While Steven was in the prison yard all alone, he thought about the next two years and how hard it was going to be with his unwanted commitment. He was determined to stay to himself because prison life was not easy. Already he had had to fight to protect himself three times. He had to watch his back because fights started all the time, gangs denominated certain areas, hideous crimes were committed, and small things became big issues. The prison environment was an education on crime, and he didn't want any part of the teaching. He focused on improving his knowledge and going to Chapel.

Steven's feelings toward his children had changed. He had had time to think and to realize all his faults and what his kids meant to him. He knew that they needed more than what he had given them thus far. With Vanessa gone, he was determined to be the father he refused to be when she was alive. He wanted to make all his wrongs right, and he could with the kids, but not with Vanessa.

For years, Steven had used the phrase "death sentence" in describing having children, marriage, and not having the freedom to come and go as he pleased. The true definition of "death sentence," he found out quickly, was being confined to four walls and not able to be free for any set time. He wanted out of this daydream. He knew any day he would wake up and find out he was only dreaming. At the telephone, he dialed the first three digits of Taffi's phone number and hung up.

The painters had painted two rooms before they took the first coffee break in the kitchen. They were relaxing, eating pastries, and drinking coffee when the telephone rang. Taffi picked it up and listened to the operator. She put her hands over the receiver and said, "This call is from an inmate in the Pine State Correctional Facility. Should I accept this call? I don't know anyone in jail." She accepted the charges and said, "Hello?" And silence filled both telephone lines for a moment.

Steven said, "Mrs. James, this is Steven Hawkins, and I want to talk with you about letting my children come see me or talk with me while I'm in prison since I have two years to do here."

Outraged she said, "They're not here right now. Your kids are at the daycare for a special craft event that started at nine this morning and lasts until 5:00 P.M.," she yelled and continued calmer, "You're their father, but I don't think it would be a good idea right now for them to see you or talk to you. They lost their mother, isn't that enough? For you to come along now, confuse them, and, when you get out, go your merry way is wrong. Can't you understand that they're trying to adjust? Seeing or talking to you can complicate their lives. Do you think that's fair to them?" Before he answered she said, "I don't want to do that to them. Not now. They have been through enough."

He responded, "If you don't allow me to see my kids, I'll have to take you to court."

"Look, Steven, I have full guardianship of your children, and I refuse to allow your selfishness to destroy three wonderful lives."

"How do you have them? I didn't sign any papers allowing you full guardianship of my children?"

"No, you didn't, but your wife did, and that's all that counts," she said.

"We'll see about that," he said as he slammed the telephone down.

She took the telephone away from her ears and said, "We'll see," and slammed the telephone down.

When she finished talking, everyone in the room was staring at her in complete silence. As Taffi wiped her hands on a towel, Kate said, "What in the world is going on daughter? Why are you talking hostile? Get yourself together."

She answered, "Mom, that evil man wants to see his children, and I don't feel it is fair for him to see them now. They have gone from having a birth mother to having me as a mom. It'll confuse them having him in their lives. He'll be in prison, and I'll have to deal with the children each time they see him. I think that's too much."

Kate said, "Taffi you're judging Steven and it's not fair to judge a person. As you loved Donald despite his weight and didn't judge him, you have to learn to love others despite their sins, faults, or outer shell. I speak for myself, but I think every kid needs their biological father in their life if they have one. I'm a prime example of a child not having a father in her life, and it caused bitterness as I got older."

Sgt. Perry said, reaching for a donut and ignoring the last statement, "They charged Steven for involuntary manslaughter in the death of Vanessa.

The prosecutor, a female, disclosed Vanessa's living conditions to the court. She didn't sugar coat a single calamity that Vanessa was going through. As she exposed all her difficult times, Steven started to cry. He probably felt grieved that she had endured the pain alone. I think he had no idea regarding her true situation. Taffi you and I heard Vanessa's recount of the accident, and, from her confession, he didn't kill her. She tripped and fell on the heel of her shoe. The prosecutor was able to convince the court that she died because of Steven's negligence from the testimony of two eyewitnesses. They stated they saw him in frenzy when he was confronting her that night. Vanessa also had scratches on her face. That was enough to convict him. The court-appointed defense counsel didn't admit Vanessa's testimony into evidence because of the stress of her medical condition. I work for the penal system, and sometimes people are placed in prison for crimes they don't commit."

Last week, Steven copped a five year plea, and got three of those years suspended, leaving him two years to do in prison.

Paul Thomas said, "Taffi, despite how a situation looks, we have to love one another. Remember to always do the right thing no matter how a situation looks."

As Taffi drank her coffee, she hadn't noticed that everyone had disappeared to finish the paint job except her. As she thought about her crummy attitude toward Steven, her mind began to focus on a conversation she had had the week before with Tina Bell about disciplining children. Tina was a childhood friend with whom Taffi had attended school all the way up to college. Tina was a scrawny, gorgeous redhead with green marbled eyes and tiny specks of freckles on her nose. Taffi talked to her often, but they got together only on special occasions because of the children. Several times, Tina had voiced her disapproval of Taffi taking in Vanessa's kids. Each time, Taffi put her in her place. Tina had decided when she was in high school, after witnessing her parent's disturbing divorce, that she would never marry or have children. Thus far, she had lived up to her promise. Her career was all she wanted, and, because of self-motivation, she had acquired a wonderful career as a hospital administrator.

Taffi thought about the picture Tina had painted about a time when she was five years old when she and her brother Tommy were playing in their living room. While they played, a vase broke. Tina's mother questioned Tommy, but he wouldn't own up to doing the crime. During the questioning, Tina started to laugh. Because she laughed, her mother believed she was the guilty one, and Tina got the spanking, although Tommy had broken the vase. Tina told her how bad she felt about getting the spanking for a crime she didn't commit.

Taffi started to cry, *Thank you Lord, for showing me my wrongdoings. Forgive me for judging.* After she composed herself, she went back to painting. When she returned to the bedroom, no one mentioned her wrongful actions.

About two hours had gone by when the phone rang, again. Taffi and Kate were in Esther's room painting along with Sgt. Perry as Paul Thomas finished Eric's room. When Taffi answered, it was Steven again. She accepted the call, changed her attitude and didn't judge him, but gave him a chance to speak.

He was sincere about wanting to do the right thing by his kids. He said, "Mrs. James, let me start over on the right foot. I've made some bad mistakes in my life, and I want to make it right with my kids. Please, may I talk with them?"

Her voice was calm, "Steven, I was telling you the truth when I said they're at a school activity and aren't here right now."

She blushed, amazed she was peaceful, and said, "Steven, I know you want to see your kids, but right now I don't feel that it's the right time because with Vanessa gone, and with them seeing you and you disappearing, it can be devastating for them. I'm thinking in particular of Jasmine because she took Vanessa's death harder. If she sees you, more harm than good can come out of it. I love your kids, and I want to do what's best for them. I hope you look outside your box and see the overall picture that I'm trying to accomplish."

A silence was on both ends for a minute. He blurted, "Yes, I see a picture of a man bitter because he was put in jail for a crime he didn't commit. In addition, I see a man that has children he wants to see, but can't. I also made mistakes and was immature, but I've grown up and now see the light. I see what counts and what's important, wherein before I was blinded."

Taffi responded calmly, "I understand the change that has occurred in your life and the urgency to make things right, but don't do it at the expense of your children. They need you Steven, but not behind bars, they don't. I feel that when you get out in two years they'll get to know you again with no problems. Meanwhile, if they ask me about you, I'll bring them to you, is that a deal? "

He looked down to the ground, paused as he viewed the jail sleeping area, and said, "Okay, Taffi, I see what you're trying to accomplish, and I hope you're right. The reason I'm going along with what you want is because I've made many bad mistakes before, and I don't need to make another one. I'll take your suggestion and not see them or fight for them because you're stability in their lives."

"Steven, I don't feel you're making a mistake. I'll send you a report once a month on their progress, and, as soon as you get out, you can come and visit them."

"Thank you for taking my kids. I appreciate it," he said.

"You don't have to thank me, because seeing them progress everyday is thanks enough," she uttered.

Taffi felt good about the decision they both had made, and she was going to live up to all her promises to him. She was hoping he would live up to his promises also.

Chapter 6

Steven Hawkins was depressed that those who were once his friends had turned their backs on him. He had no friends. The only person that kept in touch was Mrs. James, and he knew it was because she had made him a promise. He found out fast that she was a woman of her word. His inkling was that she was the right person for his kids. When she sent their report cards, his heart would light up because Jasmine and Jackie were doing outstandingly well in school. That kept him going and gave him joy. The two year exit from the prison system was slow for Steven, but he endured his time there. He looked at how far he had come and the change was remarkable. He had stopped finding fault and accepted himself. He had enrolled in college and obtained an associate's degree in business while in prison. But what hurt was that Jasmine never asked about him. *She should want to see me because she is the oldest child and would remember me above all, since I was in and out during her childhood,* he thought.

The one important lesson he learned was not to live in guilt or condemnation. At first, he was angry for paying the time for a crime he never committed, but six months later, he got over that. He realized that he wasn't an angel and hadn't been good to his wife or to his children. He had had to have a head and heart makeover to change his thinking and merciless behavior. Steven learned a lot about the Lord. What he liked most was that God didn't keep a running record of his past mistakes once he repented. God never once rejected him. He had hoped that the world was as receptive to his change. He often thought about how he mistreated Vanessa. But after serving the two years, he overcame his anger.

When Steven called and said that he was getting out of prison the following morning and wanted to see the children, Taffi was a nervous wreck. She had been a good mom to them during his absence. She felt friction would come because he had spoken about obtaining custody of the children during the first phone conversation. Steven had a right to be their father, and she had to get used to the idea.

Taffi knew that this day would come, but deep down she loathed the whole idea. He had called the day before and twice when locked up. During those calls, he had spoken about growing up and changing, but she questioned whether he had changed. Taffi's attachment to the kids had opened the door to some insecurity about the whole ordeal of Steven coming to visit them. She knew that it was fair for them to have a relationship with him. After all, he was their biological father. Paul Thomas and Sgt. Perry had become close to the kids, and they were the father figures. She wondered if they would want to go with their biological father or to stay with her.

Kate and Sgt. Perry came over to comfort Taffi and to be mediators if need be. Taffi considered herself blessed. She had to be thankful for her life. Her rural road adventure had made her a new creation. Deep down she felt a change was coming, and she would be traveling on a new road.

Sgt. Perry was a sweetheart, and she sensed he liked her, but she brushed aside his advances. He had been there for her for the past two years, and they had become close friends, almost inseparable. He refused to let her do this alone, and she appreciated everything he'd done. She hated that he didn't move on with his life and find a female companion. The park had been a breath of fresh air when she needed that time alone, and he was there to give her a break. During the Christmas holidays, he helped put toys together. When they had a pain, he would fix their hurt. And when they had school activities and needed the presence of a father, he was right there. When you saw one of them with the kids, the other was somewhere around. Many times, they had gone out, and people told them they made a nice looking couple or asked if they were husband and wife. Taffi would always chuckle because she never even considered taking their friendship any further. She was determined to get the children out the way before thinking about starting to date. She had a long time to go before they all came of age. She was content that this was her destiny, and she wanted only to please God.

Since she had four kids, she knew no man would want to take on that big responsibility. She was okay with being single for the rest of her life. Her focus was not on a man, but on Christ first and her children second. If she never married again, that was okay with her. The happiness that Donald gave her was enough to last a lifetime.

At about 9 A.M., the bell rang, and Taffi was uneasy about the whole meeting. When she opened the door, she was shocked because there stood a tall, dark-skinned, Afro-American male with a muscular medium physique, well-groomed side burns, and a mustache and goatee. He was fine. He wasn't the person she had imagined at all. Even his voice didn't give him away. All his kids had Caucasian skin tones and straight blond hair; therefore, she thought their father was Caucasian. None of Vanessa's picture collections displayed his picture. A couple of the pictures were torn in half, so she presumed they were of Steven.

Steven introduced himself, and Taffi introduced herself, Kate, and Sgt. Perry. As she spoke, Steven was amazed at the mark of beauty he saw. Taffi had wavy golden bronze hair that touched her mid-back. Her complexion was light tan, and she stood 5'6" and weighed about 120 pounds. He accepted her invitation to go inside for a while.

Taffi reflected back to Vanessa's parents, and she realized why Vanessa's family had shunned her. It all made sense now. It was a black and white issue. *It's sad that racism, in this day and time, is still an issue to some people,* she thought. Taffi had never been a racist. She loved all people and always said the color of the skin didn't matter, for the inward heart is what counts most. Color wasn't an issue for her because her mother was Caucasian, her father was Afro-American, her deceased husband was Caucasian and her daughter was bi-racial. Her lineage was a swirl of color. Taffi was surprised that he was cordial. She imagined the worst from him, yet she got the best attitude.

Will people's attitude towards racism ever change? she asked herself.

Steven paused and asked, "You're surprised that I'm Afro-American, aren't you? Don't feel bad, many people have been shocked."

Taffi nodded and blinked at him, "Yes. I am surprised because I never thought Afro-American. I thought Caucasian. You caught me off guard."

"Does my race matter?" he asked.

"No, it explains a lot about Vanessa's parents," she said.

To Taffi's surprise, Jasmine recognized him at once, but the other two children didn't. When he walked into the living room, Jasmine came over and gave him a big hug and that meant more to him than a million bucks. "Daddy, daddy," she said. "Did you know that mom went to heaven? I thought you had gone too."

Steven hugged her and smiled, pleased because he knew why she hadn't asked for him in the two year period. He kissed Jasmine's rosy cheek and said, "No, honey, I had to go somewhere for a short while, but I'm back now." After kissing her, he felt optimistic because this day was the first day of a new beginning. He was around his kids without having the urgency to run away.

Jasmine continued, "I miss mom but …" she looked up at Taffi, beamed, and said, "Mrs. James is now my new Mommy J."

Jackie and Eric were there, but they weren't on familiar terms with him. Jackie walked away, and Eric began to cry. Steven stayed with them for about two hours without the little ones adjusting to him at all.

When he left, Jasmine said to Esther and Taffi in a whisper, "That's my daddy. He made my mom cry a lot when he left. I'm glad he didn't make you cry, Mommy J." Kate and Sgt.

Perry heard her too, but neither uttered a word. They looked at one another. Sgt. Perry put his head down in shame.

The next day Steven came over unannounced, and Taffi's escorts were gone. She allowed him to come inside the house, although she was frustrated that he had showed up again. She wanted him to go away and let them alone. The children were more receptive of him. When they went down for their nap, Steven told Taffi how much he appreciated all that she had done for the kids.

She said, "I have adjusted well to my new environment with my four children, and I love it each day. I'll not wear away easy. Seven years ago, I hated having to raise Esther by myself when my husband died. I rebelled and took it out on her. This second time I refused to rebel. God has blessed me with four beautiful kids. I have joy overflowing as I watch them grow," Kate said with poise.

She said, "While in prison, I had to grow up fast. I learned to love the Lord and to love what he blessed me with in life. I've changed, Mrs. James, and would enjoy having my ki…." When he spoke the words, he noticed her body language and realized that he was in a territory that could well begin a war. He changed the subject because he was determined to have a relationship with his children until he regained custody, and she was his only resource. He refused to blow it early in the game.

She interrupted and told him, "Steven, call me by my first name. It's Taffi."

He responded, "Okay."

As they talked, she tried not to judge him, but to see him for the person he was. To her surprise, she found him to be a humorous, yet sensitive man who lacked patience. She was surprised that he talked about Christ. He was not the man that Vanessa had described, and she was waiting for the monster to show up. Maybe he had changed for the better, but time would tell.

Chapter 7

It was Steven's one-week release from prison anniversary, and he was thinking that he had been better off in prison than dealing with the rejection he was enduring outside the four walls. He understood why many ex-cons ended up back in prison. Because they didn't have a chance to swim, they often sank back to their old habits. Steven had tried everything to get a job, but nothing was happening. He couldn't go far because walking was his form of transportation. Many times, he had stormed out of local businesses when they refused him. But today his frustrations got the best of him. He headed to Taffi's house, not knowing if she would be there since it was a workday for her. He was happy that at last he had a true friend. Not expecting a response, he knocked on the door. She opened the door after the second knock. When she looked out at him, a breeze of incense swept the atmosphere. He said, "I didn't anticipate you to be home today. I was troubled and stopped by hoping to find you."

"Well you're in time for lunch, would you care for any?"

He nodded, "I don't know if I have an appetite for food right now."

With pleasure she said, "By the way, you're lucky that I answered the door because I took off half a day to catch up on some work that I've been putting off. But I have a few minutes to spare, since I put the younger children down for a nap and the older children are still at school. Have a seat while I arrange these sandwiches on a plate."

He started to pace the floor. "May I vent my frustrations to you? I need to talk, and I have no one else to talk to but you."

"I'm here," she said as she opened a bag of chips and arranged them on the plates along with the sandwiches.

"Taffi, did you know that once you're in the penal system, people lose respect for you. I have tried to get a job with no luck. People don't care. They looked at me as though I'm a thug. Once a thug, always a thug. I'd do more with my life, but society won't give me a second chance now that I've been jailed. When I get an application for a job, the one question asked is whether you've ever been arrested for a felony or a misdemeanor. When I say yes, attitudes change." He sat next to her, smiled, and said, "In reality, I'm a nice guy Taffi."

She teased, "Uh! Maybe you are."

Steven smiled and said, "You, perhaps, would beg to differ, since I've been convicted of involuntary manslaughter. But believe me I committed no crime. I never killed my own wife. I loved Vanessa, but I was too immature to admit it or show it. I had to play the player because being tied down, I felt old or henpecked. I've made some stupid choices in life that have caused demise, but I deserve a second chance. How long is the train going to run on my tracks without stopping? I have paid my debt to society, a debt that should not have been paid in the first place."

"Steven, you must move on with your life and forgive society for hurting you. Maybe being in jail allowed God to work His plan for your life. Remember, you weren't living the ideal lifestyle He would approve of. In prison, you were able to see the light shining to guide you in the right direction. No one ever said that the road would be easy, but you still have to press forward." She added, "If you knew half of my story and the rural road journey I've had to take, you wouldn't complain. My journey is smooth driving now, but I've had some ups and some downs also. Yes, you're having a hard time now, but the curves and bumps on the road will lighten up some. Before long, you'll be at your destiny if you don't quit or travel the wrong road."

She threw a probing look and said, "You perhaps haven't thought about this, but look at the rural roads your wife had to drive on." He looked disdained by the comment, but she continued, "Life is full of bumpy rural roads. The key is managing rural driving. First, your visibility must be maintained, which is keeping your vision clear by setting goals. What's needed is watching out, reducing speed, and allowing extra time on rural roads, which means keeping focused." She grabbed a pear from the fruit bowl, cut it in half and said, "Last of all, space on the roads must be maintained by allowing for reaction time, following distance, passing, and other distractions, which means you have to position yourself for success. Once you maintain these three areas in your life, success is in the making."

"How is that when the same thing occurs every time I go fill out job application, and it asks the same question? Have you ever been convicted of a crime? Once I mark yes, the employer looks at it, and, boom! The application is denied. Taffi, the system takes you in a vicious cycle with no recourse. What's hurtful is that I committed no crime, but I'm still paying for a crime I never committed."

"Maybe you haven't given it a chance. You've been out a week and haven't had time to get frustrated yet," she said with precision.

He continued acknowledging the truth, "You're right. I should give it some time, but it's hard when you have no money. I was used to living on my own, and having to live with my mother again is not fun. I went back to my old job, but they said my position was filled, and they wouldn't hire me back even on a temporary basis. When you're down-and-out, so-called friends disappear. To top it off, my mom sold my truck to help pay off my outstanding bills. I'm in a big mess, and the one positive thing I have right now is coming to see my children. I love that children have no care in the world. And they love you, despite how messed up you are on the inside."

She picked up a pear and said, "There is one positive thing, and that's Jesus. He never left you, but carried you along the way through your tragedy, and He'll carry you into triumph now. I'll talk to my father and see what he can do to help you out of your dilemma, but I'm not promising you anything."

He said, "That's more than anyone else has done. Thanks."

Paul Thomas loved being a servant to others, and he treated all people honorably whether they were honorable or not. He was a man of love and did things not to be appreciated, but because he loved. When Taffi called him and told him Steven's situation, Paul Thomas, without hesitation, told her that he would hire Steven and that he had a place for him to stay.

Taffi had given him the shelter's address, called her father, and told him he was coming. She loved the work that her family did, because it ended in positive results.

Steven went to the church main office and filled out an application for formalities purposes. He asked the secretary if he'd be able to speak with Paul Thomas. The secretary told him that Pastor Thomas was busy organizing some business papers. Steven told her that he knew he was coming, so the secretary called him on the phone, and Paul Thomas told her he would see him.

When Steven entered the office, he noticed three walls full of certificates of appreciation from work done in the community. Although the room was quiet and peaceful, the loud sound of the deeds of good work permeated throughout the room. Paul Thomas was on the floor looking at papers spread out everywhere when Steven entered. Had the papers not been on the floor, the office would've been clean. "How may I help you?" Paul Thomas asked.

Steven was apprehensive as he answered, "I'm Steven, a friend of your daughter, and she spoke to you about a job and living situation for me. She told me to stop by and that you'd help me out."

"Hey son, I've been waiting for you," Paul Thomas said and extended his hand. Steven shook his hand. "Excuse the mess, but I'm trying to figure something out."

"May I be of service to you, sir?" Steven asked.

"Uh!" Paul Thomas said as he scratched his head, "Maybe you.... Come on down here and see what I'm trying to do." When Steven got in close proximity, he pointed to the paperwork,

"These are all the businesses that I have, and I'm trying to compile them in some type order and to find a budget for each one. If you do this for me, we'll be friends forever. My assistant quit two weeks ago. She was moving to Kansas with her spouse, and I've been working on these papers since yesterday afternoon with no results."

Steven asked him a couple questions about each business and was able to compile each in order from most important to least important. He composed a budget for each one. It took him about one hour, and he was finished. Paul Thomas was impressed with his exemplary work. He said to Steve, "Son, you're hired as my administrative assistant, but there is one prerequisite. You must be saved to work in this church. Do you know the Lord, or have you accepted Him as your Savior?"

"Pastor Thomas, I have learned a lot about the Lord while in prison, and, though I believe in Him and know that He is the way, the truth, and the life, I've never committed myself to Him," he said truthful.

"Well son, I think there's not a better time than now. What do you think?"

"Yes sir, there's not a better time than now." Steven accepted Jesus as his Savior and repented his sins. The presence of God filled the office.

Paul Thomas continued to talk, "Son, now that you have confessed your faith, there are steps that are required to help you live a successful everyday Christian life. Be baptized, worship Christ, become intimate with Him, love your neighbor, and attend a church that preaches Jesus. You don't have to attend here, although you're welcomed here. Are you willing to do all those things?"

"Pastor Thomas, I have a question to ask before I answer you. What does become intimate with him mean?"

"Intimacy means getting close by chatting or touching Him through prayer, fasting, learning, and reading the Word to become familiar with Him. I'll be baptizing you on this coming Sunday night."

"You have a deal. I'm able to do this," he said and smiled at Pastor Thomas.

"I feel confident that you're the right person for the job. In the position of administrative assistant, you'll work along side me. You'll be in charge of making sure everything runs smoothly in my office. There's one more point you need to know — God is the head boss here, and we'll do what ever He tells us to do. That means we have to fast and pray. I'll put the distinguishing seal of approval on all decisions once I get confirmation from God. "

"Pastor Thomas what's your congregation going to say when they find out that I'm an ex-convict?" he asked, looking sad.

"If there's any man without sin, let him cast the first stone. We've all sinned and fallen short. There are people in the Bible who went to prison and were ex-cons. Moses killed a solider, Peter cut off the ear of a soldier, and Joseph went to prison, not to mention that the Apostle John, Samson, and Jeremiah were prisoners. In addition, Jesus Christ happened to go to jail before execution. Our job is not to judge, but to support a person, no matter what they do. No one should say anything.

"The rule required to stay in the shelter is to attend at least two motivational classes per week given by the shelter. Are you willing to follow the rules?" Pastor Thomas asked.

"Yes sir, I'm willing to follow the rules," he said. He signed the agreement and moved in that night at the shelter. Everything turned around in no time, and his life was getting straight. He had agreed that if he violated the rules, it was grounds for expulsion from the job and the shelter. More than anything, he loved the idea that he was in reach of his children.

It took until Sunday for him to settle into his new environment and the rules. Everyday, he made sure he visited his children. Time went by fast, and his baptism was at seven o'clock. Steven invited his mother, Taffi, Sgt. Perry, Esther and his children. He became good friend with Sgt. Perry. Taffi saw a noticeable change in Steven's attitude. He stopped focusing on suing and became dutiful to getting the tasks done that Pastor Thomas had assigned him.

Before 7:00 P.M., Steven showed up at the church with his change of clothing. He was anxious to take the required steps and had prepared to give his declaration of faith. Steven was the only adult scheduled for the baptism, along with five children. The congregation was smaller than usual because it was a Sunday evening service, and not many people supported the service. On his turn for public confession, he was nervous, but kept going. He looked out in the audience, and, on the first row in front of him, sat his whole family. His nervousness turned into delight as he began to smile. Steven said, "I have never been baptized before. Two years ago, I would have never taken the steps I'm taking now to get closer to God. For many years, it has been all about me. I was prideful, self-centered, and lacked moral values, and my action denoted that fact. But, I had time to think. Life and family is what's important to me. God looked down on my wrecked old soul and gave me a second chance." He pointed to himself and continued, "I was surrounded with positive people that didn't look at my faults with judgment, but they looked at me as a person with potential." He looked up, "God, I repent for my sins, for I am a sinner. I'm doing this as a confession of my faith in You. I love you, Lord, and you are my God."

Chapter 8

It was the first day of spring, and the birds outside were chirping away in a large beautiful oak tree in Taffi's front yard. Some of the birds were in the yard pulling worms out the ground. Taffi looked out and knew that wintertime was over because it was bright outside and all the darkness had fled. The wind was blowing, but no more heavy winter coats just a nice thin jacket was fine. The animals, birds, plants, and insects were beginning to appear everywhere. Springtime meant a time of change, watering, and growth. Taffi was bouncing back since winter was gone. She felt that this spring was going to be amazing.

Adam and Joseph hadn't stopped coming by to see the kids. In spite of everything, they knew if their father caught them, they would be in for a whipping. But he never found out, and they kept coming for two years. They had called and said they wanted to take the children to the park at 11 A.M. since springtime had sprung and the weather was nice. They loved their nieces and nephew, and, a few times, they even purchased gifts and toys for them. Joseph was in college, and Adam was a senior in high school. Taffi always welcomed them, and the kids approved of their visits. Sometimes Steven would stop over while the brothers were visiting. Her brothers had no qualms with him, and they got along fine.

Jennifer's sons told their mom every time they visited Taffi to report on what each child was doing. Although, Jennifer did not interact with her grandchildren, she knew each one by name, and she knew the certain traits they had from listening to her sons. Jennifer was a well-respected person in the community as well as her Earl. They owned a local sports bar, and it was successful. Weekly, however, she got a beating from him. Not only did she conceal it, but she also did a good job of it. He had got to the point where he didn't hit her on her face, but everywhere else that wasn't visible to the eye. She was tired of the beatings, but stuck around, since he begged her not to run off because of his standing within the community. Since she had no self-esteem or courage and her sons needed a father, she stayed married to him.

Earl had served Jennifer divorce papers and moved out over the past weekend. Jennifer was happy because she didn't know how to get rid of him. He was a controlling man, and she was tired of dealing with him. They had been married for thirty years, which she thought was too long because the flame had died out long ago. The reason she had stuck around was that her sons still were in school. Now, the last one was graduating in a couple months, and she was ready to make a change. She informed Earl that whatever he wanted was his, as long as she got the house.

A long time ago, Jennifer started setting aside money that she had invested for her departure, but she had been too scared to ditch him. Last week, she visited her investor who told her that she was a rich woman. She never let Earl know her financial status. If she had revealed it, he would have stuck around to help her deplete the investments, or he would have taken it all away from her and did what he pleased.

Earl was a bigot, recognized throughout the community as a nice person. He called Vanessa a traitor for turning to the black race when she started dating Steven. When she approached him with the news of getting married to Steven after graduating from high school, Earl gave her a narrow-minded speech. He said, "You're going to live as one. Watch and see that low life won't do nothing but bring you down. I hate them, and, because you're marrying one, I hate you too. Vanessa, you're making your bed, and you're going to lay in it, too. I have nothing for white women that go for black men. You disgust this family and me, and, if you marry him, from this day forward we'll have nothing to do with you. If you ever have children, I'll never love your black children. I hate blacks." Vanessa left that day and married Steven on the following day.

Earl had forbidden Jennifer, Adam, and Joseph from having anything to do with Vanessa. Jennifer wasn't against Vanessa because one time she had dated an Afro-American man before dating Earl, but she kept that fact a secret. To keep peace within the household, she complied with his decision to shun their daughter. She wanted to visit her grandchildren following Vanessa's death, but Earl dared her to step foot on Taffi's land.

Jennifer decided to visit her grandchildren on this perfect change of season. She was free and taking control. She had an appointment at the hairdresser, and, afterward, she was heading to see them. She longed to get up close enough to hug and kiss them. At the funeral, she was close to putting her hands on them, but she had to get away right after the funeral. He hadn't allowed her to stay for the burial.

She squeezed her eyes shut tightly and thought about the day she got the call from Sgt. Perry telling her that Vanessa was in the hospital. Her mind replayed that day because she spoke up for the first time, even though in the end she weakened and gave in to his mediocrity.

She was sitting on the sofa when the phone rang. Earl told her to get the phone. When she answered, Sgt. Perry asked her if her daughter's name was Vanessa Hawkins. She responded with a yes, and he proceeded to explain the situation. Jennifer took the phone away from her ear, placed it on her heart, and started to cry.

Earl asked hatefully, "What are you crying about now? All you do is bawl about nothing."

She turned to look at him and replied, "It's Vanessa. She's in the hospital in bad shape. They don't know if she'll make it through the night, and I'm going to see her, right now."

He was quick to point out, "We won't go and visit her. Let her black relatives watch over her."

She continued with confidence, "She's my daughter, and I'll go, with or without you. " She has your and my white bloodline flowing through her veins. She needs me now, and I'm going." She couldn't believe that she was brave and firm with him.

He nodded and held her hand firmly, "No Jennifer, I won't allow you to see her."

She managed to break loose, crying, "She's my daughter. I'm going to the hospital." She ran out the house and drove off.

He followed her to the hospital, and when she parked, he blocked her in and ran out of his car. He grabbed her arm, slapped her face, and said, "Jennifer, I have a reputation to uphold in this community, and if you go in, I'll lose my standing. We have two other mouths to feed. Is she worth all that? I won't let you blow it for me. Face it, she's made her bed with that black man, and I warned her that he would bring her down." Looking at her, livid, he said, "We have to go before we're seen." He raised his hand up to hit her again. "I won't lose my reputation, Jennifer. I've come too far."

Weeping she asked, "May I go in and find out her status? She's my daughter, and I love her."

He spit out the beef jerky juice and said, "No, she was our daughter, but now she is a black man's wife. We won't stay long, just long enough to get her status. Is that understood?"

She said, "Yes," and was about to say more, but stopped.

She hated leaving Vanessa in the hospital. Earl refused to let her stay. He told Jennifer that if she didn't hurry, he would beat her to smithereens whenever she returned home. To avoid a beating, she left with him and left her daughter to die.

When Earl found out that Vanessa had died, he told Jennifer not to think about getting her children because he wanted no black children living in his home. And if a situation ever happened, it would be over his dead body. Jennifer went along with him to keep peace, but she hated not hugging or touching her grandchildren.

But on this day, Jennifer went to Taffi's home with many wrapped gifts in her hands. She'd decided not to call, but make a surprise visit in case something happened with Earl so that Taffi wouldn't be waiting for her. Jennifer knocked with her free hand,

and Taffi answered the door and said, "Mrs. Moore, I..." she smiled and motioned to her, "Come on in."

"Taffi, I want to see my grandchildren, please," she said and swallowed hard.

"Mrs. Moore, they'll be back in about ten minutes. Your sons took them to the park today."

"What? They knew what time I was coming over here today. Maybe this is a setup to give us time to talk."

"Yes, maybe you're right Mrs. Moore."

"Taffi, I've been stupid all these years to be controlled by a hateful, evil man. He used his control to destroy wonderful relationships." She started to cry, "Why was I stupid?"

Taffi reached for a tissue, "Mrs. Moore, do you love the Lord?"

She responded, "Yes, I do, and I go to church every Sunday and have since Vanessa was a toddler. Because of our business and keeping up our reputation, we have always gone to church. But sometimes I've gone bruised from my neck down to my knees from the beatings."

"To control or to attempt to influence a person to believe what you believe is wrong. Moreover, racism is injustice and a sin. Although you didn't hold it in your heart, you allowed your husband to execute a repulsive act on your daughter and you didn't stop him. When you acted alongside him and performed the same acts on your daughter and her children as he did, then you were an accomplice to a hideous sin. You have identified racism as your sin. Repent or confess and turn away from it and ask for forgiveness. God will be faithful to forgive you of your sins. He is that type God. The Word says, 'You should be a keeper of peace and get along with one another.' Also, it states, 'Love your neighbor as yourself.' How do you love the Lord, go to church, and hate your brother?"

Jennifer apologized, "Taffi, I'm sorry of all the wrong doing I've done."

"Be sorrowful to God, not me. I hate to be the bearer of bad news, but if you serve God, the One that starts with a capital letter 'G,' not the one that starts with a small 'g,' you must get rid of all forms of racism. There's no such thing as small sin versus large sin. Sin is sin, no matter what. When you sin, you don't please God. Sin makes God angry. Even when you repent of racism, but don't turn away and continue to do or say the bad things you use to say, you're still walking in sin. Here's an example that happened to me. I visited a friend in a college dormitory, and she had a roommate who loved to cook their meals. I looked at the roommate, and she was of Asian decent. I asked, 'Where are you from, Korea? And is Korean food the type food you cook?' She was adamant and answered, 'No, my mom is from Thailand, and my dad is American, and I love cooking all sorts of foods.' The question I asked was discriminatory, and after I asked it, conviction came upon me. See how simple it is to sin with your mouth? I had to repent."

"I never looked at it that way, but I guess it is sin."

"Mrs. Moore, you have a set of fine grandchildren, and I love them to death. God has no respect of person, and we have to be more like Him. When you look at those beautiful grandchildren of yours, love them, and look at them as God does, with no color. Is it all right if we pray before they come back?"

Jennifer nodded her head with tears in her eyes and said, "Yes, we can."

Taffi held her hands, *"Dear Lord, You are my Savior. We're coming to you, asking that You do a work in Mrs. Moore's life. Lord, help her to build her self-esteem up. Help her during these times of change. Allow her to build a relationship with her grandchildren and her son-in-law. Most of all, teach her not to demonstrate racism but to teach her grandchildren to love all people, people of all shades, disabilities and sizes. Lord, there are many hurting people in this world because people say or do hurtful things to them. Help us to humble ourselves and be kind to one another. Lord, she has identified racism as a sin that she performed. Forgive her Lord of this hurtful sin. Allow her to turn away from it. Help Jasmine, Jackie, and Eric to be receptive to their new grandmother. Amen."*

When the kids returned, Taffi had their lunch prepared. She waited while they washed their hands. When they came past the living room, she told them that she wanted to talk to them. Jasmine returned first, and she started talking about the outing while Adam and Joseph took a seat in the living room.

"Hi, Mommy J," she waved her hand. "We had fun learning how to jump rope, and I did it, too."

Taffi responded to her, as the rest of the gang strolled in and took their seats. Taffi said, "Today, we have a special guest visiting us. Jasmine, Jackie, and Eric, welcome your Grandma Moore." They all said hi, as they looked at her hard. Jasmine asked, "How's she be my grandma?"

"It's easy Jasmine, your mother had a mother, and she is your Grandma Moore."

Jasmine scratched her head, "My mom told me that her mother was too sick and that we would never meet her. And she said she loved her with all her heart."

Grandma Moore glanced at Taffi and smiled as she continued, "I loved your mommy, too, and she was right, because I was sick. I love you all and want to be in your lives now. Is that all right with you?"

Jasmine responded, "Yes, you may be in our lives."

"Thank you, Jasmine," she said, and she gave them all a kiss and hug. She wanted to hug them forever. They were beautiful, little children. She had come close to missing the chance to know her darling grandchildren. Once the embracing was over, she handed them all a gift. She had learned many valuable lessons, but the greatest one was to love children of a different colors. She would never be the same because she was now a genuine grandmother who was no longer ashamed that they were part Afro-American.

As she was getting ready to head off, Steven had stopped by, and she was able to face him and apologize for being prejudiced against him. When she looked at him, she saw that he was a handsome man that had a great deal more pigment than she had. He was a human being. She said to him, "Black, white, yellow, purple, red, we're all God's children. This has been a time of growth for me. I claimed to be a Christian, and I held anguish in my heart toward people because of the color of their skin. In doing it, I've sinned."

Reaching for the door handle, she said, "Taffi, you're the first person to show me the light on racism. I'll never be the same again because I'm changed. I'll now press forward to do the right thing regarding people with a different color."

Chapter 9

Summertime for the past two years had been busy for Taffi since she had the four children. She worked part-time during the summer months until school started back again. Sgt. Perry had taken two-week's vacation to help her and Steven. To her surprise, Mrs. Moore offered to keep all the children for one-month. The time flew by with both the older girls on different summer basketball leagues. Jackie was taking reading and swimming classes. Eric wasn't doing much except being an ornery little two-year-old boy who was beginning to show everyone his independence.

At the end of August, the two older kids went back to elementary school, and Jackie went to kindergarten for half days. Taffi thought she was going to get a break from sports activities during the fall season until Esther voiced an interest in swimming. Before joining the swim team, Esther had to take swim lessons and try out for the team. In mid-September, the swim classes began, and, of course, Jasmine joined too.

Taffi was grateful that instead of one two males were always around, and sometimes three, if Paul Thomas showed up. They were great at relieving some of the pressures of having all the children around. They were a help in time of need and they often took the girls to practice while Taffi stayed at home with the younger kids.

Esther was seven years old and was a beautiful girl. She had the prettiest light blue eyes that were as bright as the blue sky, she had long curly golden bronze hair, and her skin tone was pale, comparable to her fathers. She was beautiful, no different from her mom or her grandmother. She was in the second grade and loved it. Taffi observed Donald in her. Esther had his eyes and his skin tone, and she was starting to get as pudgy as him. She had Taffi's hair color and facial appearances. Esther displayed the act of giving, as her father and Taffi loved that. She was a super girl that loved the Lord. Everything Paul Thomas taught her about the Bible she remembered. He had stated once that maybe she would be a pastor one day, and Taffi agreed. She was a wonderful child, and she loved her new sisters and brother. Esther and Jasmine made perfect sisters, and they did everything together.

They were in their second week of swim lessons and went three times a week. When they came home, the strokes had exhausted them both. It was a Friday night, and the girls had swim classes at 6:30 P.M. After school, Esther took a nap around four in the afternoon. When Taffi tried to awaken her, she wouldn't wake up. Since Taffi felt that Esther was tired from the swimming, she let her sleep and had Sgt. Perry take Jasmine to the lesson without her. When Esther woke up, it was 8:00 P.M. the next morning, and the church was having a play. Esther was in the play and had invited Sgt. Perry and Steven, along with the rest of the gang. At 6:00 P.M., they all were in Taffi's van, and the grandparents were meeting them there. Esther was playing a leaf, and she was proud that she knew her part. Before she went on stage, she went to the restroom. While on stage, Esther left the stage to go to the restroom. It was time for her to say her part, but she missed it, and the director motioned for the next actor to say his part. Taffi ran back stage once she saw that Esther was there. She thought that maybe she had stage fright. Nevertheless, she found out that Esther needed a potty break. Right after the restroom break, she stopped at the water fountain and drank a lot of water. Esther went back on stage. Near the end of the play during the grand finale, Esther had the urgency to go to the restroom again. She left the stage as Taffi had returned to her seat.

Steven mentioned, "Esther sure is going to the bathroom a lot."

Kate said, "She sure is. Maybe it's nerves."

After the play, Steven took the Esther and Jasmine to a football game. Esther slept all the way in the car to the football game. He noticed that Esther was going to the bathroom a lot at the game, the same as at the play. When he took her back home, he mentioned the unusual frequency to Taffi.

Taffi told him that she would take her to the doctor the following week. The next day after church, Esther ate a corndog for lunch. When she went to the bathroom, she looked at her tongue and white swelling hairy bumps covered it. She ran to Taffi and said, "Mom, look at my tongue."

Taffi looked into her mouth and phoned the doctor. The doctor said, "Go to the emergency room, the symptoms you described, tiredness, excessive thirst, and frequent urination might need to be treated with insulin. When you go to the hospital, tell them everything that you've told me."

Taffi hurried and put on her shoes and took Esther to the hospital. Steven and Sgt. Perry had gone with her to church. Right after the service, Sgt. Perry had duty and left. Steven stayed with the children.

The packed emergency room had people of all ages sitting around, waiting like cattle to herd out of there. Some had head, eye, arm, or leg injuries. Some were talking, and some were too sick to talk. Some watched the television. Some were sleeping, and some were reading magazines. Some of the patients were outside smoking cigarettes or talking on cell phones. There was an ambulance by the emergency exit. Two clerks were at the front desk, and the others were busy with the patients coming in from the ambulance. Taffi wished she didn't have to be there. She hated hospitals. She had been lucky because this was the first time in months having to visit the emergency room, especially with four children. Hours had passed by, before the triage nurse called them. Taffi told her all of Esther's symptoms. The nurse escorted them to a room and gave Esther a hospital gown to put on. Once dressed, she lounged on the bed as Taffi sat by her side. Esther played with the bed controls and asked all sort questions. As they waited for the doctor, Taffi found out there had been a bad accident in which three people were injured and one had died.

"Mom, nothing is wrong with me. I feel okay. May we go home now?"

Taffi said, "I know baby, but we're getting you checked out to be on the safe side." Time appeared to stop. The emergency room doctor came and spoke to Esther and ordered a lot of tests. Minutes later, a male lab technician came into the room to draw blood. Taffi rose and stood by Esther's bedside, holding her hand as the technician drew nine tubes of blood. He pricked Esther's finger and put the dropping of blood on a strip, in a monitor. Taffi didn't know a lot about blood sugar levels, but she glanced at the monitor awaiting the results, knowing it would be normal. The technician began to speak, but before he said a word, Taffi started to cry because she saw the numbers. It displayed 445, and she knew that a normal blood sugar level was 80-120. As Taffi started to cry, it made Esther cry too, although she didn't know why she was crying. Taffi gave her a huge hug. A nurse came in to start an IV, and she asked for a urine specimen.

Sgt. Perry called Taffi's house, and Steven told him what was going on with Esther. He stopped by to see them at the hospital. He entered the room, and Taffi was crying. He escorted her to the hallway and asked her why she was crying. He held her and asked, "Taffi where's your faith? You have to be strong for Esther because if she sees you crying, she'll cry, and that's not what is needed now." He wiped every tear from her face with a tissue. "I'm here for you if you need me, okay?"

She nodded after realizing that he was right. She needed to pull herself together for Esther's sake. They returned to the room, but as soon as she saw Esther, she started to cry again. Esther asked, "Mom are you crying because I'm going to die like Jasmine's mom?"

"No honey, it's… your… blood sugar levels. They are high."

Thereafter, the physician came into the room. He asked Taffi, "Why are you crying?" Taffi looked at him as he continued, "Your daughter has diabetes, and will be transported to Ports Children's Hospital in a couple of hours" Ports Children's Hospital was familiar ground for Taffi because Esther had been a patient there as an infant. She never thought she would ever have to take her back as a patient again. The doctor continued, "One of my best friend's daughters was diagnosed with diabetes and she's on the pump and doing fine," he said on his way out of the room. How he spoke brought tears to Taffi's eyes. He was cold and uncaring. And it wasn't the report that she wanted to hear.

As Taffi, cried Esther did too. Sgt. Perry went over to Esther and held her. Taffi left the room to pull herself together and to call her parents and Steven to inform them of the negative report.

Taffi said, "No, this can't be happening." She stepped into the hallway as if a zombie. She made the telephone calls and went back into the room with Esther. Sgt. Perry was still holding Esther, but she had stopped crying when Taffi returned. She knew that she had to pull herself together so that she wouldn't make her cry again. She kissed and hugged Esther and said, "Honey, I love you. The doctor has given us a bad report. He says you have a disease called diabetes."

"What is that, mom?"

"It's a disease that requires you to take shots everyday because the pancreas stops producing insulin. Our bodies need insulin to keep the blood sugar levels normal. The medication found in the needles is insulin, which is a protein substitute for the missing insulin your body doesn't produce at the right levels. You'll have to eat the correct amount of carbohydrates for each meal. Diabetes, if not managed, will cause serious complications later in life."

Within minutes, Paul Thomas and Kate were at the hospital. They came right in the room. They wanted to know if everything was all right with their granddaughter. Taffi explained what was going on. They waited in the room in silence as the nurse came in to check the intravenous drip and to take Esther's blood pressure and her temperature.

Kate told Esther, "Everything is going to be fine." She and Paul Thomas said a prayer for Esther.

Within the next couple of hours, they were on the way to Ports Children's Hospital. The ride was a joy to Esther because she had never ridden in an ambulance before. As she looked out the small window, she saw the big world outside, but it hadn't turned to darkness. Taffi looked puzzled that all this was happening to her daughter. She wanted to turn back the hands of time and prevent this part of her life from happening. Nevertheless, the reality was that it was happening, and she felt out of control regarding the whole circumstance. She felt the enemy had her, and she didn't have a fight. On the other hand, she knew that if God allowed it, He would open another door of healing.

When Esther arrived at Ports Children's Hospital, they took her to a room. They ordered more tests and continued to give her insulin to bring her sugar levels down.

Esther and Taffi stayed in the hospital for three days learning about diabetes. They learned how to give the insulin injections. Esther's endocrinologist, nurse practitioner, dietitian, and education specialist visited her each day. Before they left the hospital, they were able to count carbohydrates and give insulin injections.

Taffi never asked the Lord why, because she believed one day her daughter would get her healing. When they got home, Steven was in the kitchen fixing sandwiches. He had stayed at Taffi's house while she was at the hospital to take care of his children. The week seemed long to him, but he stuck it out. He didn't know if he would be able to be a father on a full-time basis, but with Taffi gone, things went smoothly, and he didn't want to run off. He felt these feelings were because he felt obligated to Taffi or maybe because he had changed. Once she got back, he was ready with his bags at the door, waiting to make an exit. His kids were good kids, but he figured that he was the problem.

The transition of caring for a child with diabetes was at times overbearing. Taffi continued to pray for her healing. Esther had a normal life, and she did everything as before except her eating times had changed, with the amounts of foods and the three injections. Taffi was thankful that she never complained about having to give herself the injections. When she was in her goal range of 80-180, she was fine. The problem occurred when the sugar levels were above or below the range. When her blood sugar levels were high, she had Esther force fluids, and when it came down enough, she would take her to exercise. When they were low, she gave her more carbohydrates to eat. When it was low, it caused her to be shaky, cranky, thirsty, and dizzy. With the high blood sugar level, she was sleepy and cranky, and she urinated a lot.

Taffi thought about Esther's name and the meaning of it. Despite all that was going on, she knew that God was the answer. And the reason she had come this far. Taffi remembered the Sunday when she entered the flowing river of revival and realized that her destiny was to love God first and others. Her dad had shown her the meaning of Esther's name. He had said that Esther was a gift from God, and she believed him. Esther's presence in Taffi's life allowed light to shine on the darkness, as if Esther was a star. Paul Thomas had said that Esther's name would be a reminder for her to get in the presence of God.

The illness was darkness, but Esther's light still shined. Esther was always in good spirits, allowing her light to shine bright even when she was in the hospital. Taffi thought she needed to get back in the presence of God because He was the common denominator that was missing.

One month had passed and everyone had adjusted to helping Esther overcome the obstacles. Taffi received a letter from the endocrinologist stating,

Dear Mrs. James,

Esther's test results regarding the type diabetes have returned: islet cell antibody positive 163840 units and anti-GAD antibodies positive at greater than thirty. These test results, coupled with the low C-peptide level, indicate that Esther has Type 1 Diabetes.

Taffi put the letter on the refrigerator and wrote on it, *Esther is already healed of this disease.*

Taffi had started reading the Bible, and when she came across Jesus in the upper room, she felt compelled to partake of Communion until Esther's healing manifested. Every morning Taffi and Esther would self-examine themselves for the right attitude and right approach before taking Communion. They repented for their sins and prayed, *Thank You, Lord, for this opportunity to break bread with You. This bread represents Your body, Jesus, Yeshua the Messiah, the Lamb of God that takes away the sin of the world. You said to do this in remembrance of You. This cup represents Your blood shed on Calvary for eternal salvation for us. 'This cup, which is poured out for you, is the new covenant in My blood.' God, You were wounded for my transgressions, bruised for my iniquities, and by Your stripes Esther is already healed. I believe that your blood is blessed. By the authority of the Word, loose Esther and set her free from diabetes. In Jesus Name.*

During nighttime prayer, Taffi and Esther would hold hands and say, *Die diabetes, and by His stripes, I'm healed. I'm the righteousness of God and already healed. Thank You, Lord for my healing.* Although she didn't receive the healing right away, they continued to pray and have Communion every day and to live holy because, one day, they knew they would rejoice over Esther's healing. Taffi had no doubt in her mind.

Steven came by every day to help Taffi. He was there for breakfast, and he would return for dinner and stay until after Esther's evening snack. Even on the weekends, he was there supporting her. Sgt. Perry stopped by too. She felt joy in her heart that she didn't have to do this alone. She had two great friends in Sgt. Perry and Steven. She loved them, and the kids did too.

Chapter 10

Everyday Sgt. Perry stopped by to check on Taffi and the kids, and it was a day-by-day ritual since Vanessa's hospitalization. He was a dedicated, wonderful friend, and Taffi loved him dearly. She never looked at him beyond being a friend though. In all their years of being acquainted, he never made advances toward her. She often wondered why he stuck close around her and the kids. Taffi had often hinted to him that whoever got him as a mate was getting a super fellow. And he would chuckle, "I know that."

One cold snowy morning, Eric was looking out the window at the snow. He yelled, "Sgt. Perry! Sgt. Perry!" and all the kids scurried toward the door to greet him. They loved him and his loud playful voice. Sgt. Perry heard them playing hide-and-seek and ran toward them. He ran through the house acting as if he didn't see them, and, after a while, he started finding them and calling out their names. He fell to the ground as they all jumped on him. Taffi smiled at the laughter and enjoyment they were having early in the morning. He had more fun than the children did and was a kid at heart.

After they played and the children went their merry way, Sgt. Perry whispered in Taffi's ear, "I want to talk with you later." As soon as the kids ate lunch, Taffi put them down for a nap. She and Sgt. Perry went into the living room, and he looked worried as he said, "Taffi, I've known you for a long time and I . . . " he stopped talking to clear his throat. " I'm sorry about that. Let me start over since we've been best friends for a long time, and I discern that the children care for me, and I love them too. I have thought hard about what I'm about to say to you." He knelt on his knees and said, "I would love to be the father of your children and your husband. Taffi, will you marry me?"

She glanced at him shocked and said nothing. He reached into his shirt pocket and pulled out a ring. He said, "I think it'll be nice for them to have a permanent father figure around here, what you think?" he asked.

Still surprised she squeezed her eyes shut tightly, thinking. After a couple minutes he asked, "Does that mean yes or no?"

"Well, I never looked at you as someone to marry because we have always been best friends. Why ruin our wonderful friendship with marriage when we love one another as if we're sister and brother? That wouldn't be fair to either of us, nor the children."

He said, "I adore the way you care for the kids and how you're kind and generous to people. There's not one thing I've seen that I dislike about you. I would love to live the rest of my life with you and your children. Even if there's no love connection, it'll grow to be one day, perhaps."

"Sgt. Perry," she started as he interrupted.

"Please don't call me Sgt. Perry. You know me as David."

"David, I'll have to think about getting married again. Donald's been dead for seven years now, and I've never thought about remarriage."

"While you're working it out, what will your answer be?"

"Let me give my answer later on tonight, okay?" she said.

"Sure, I'll give you until that time, Taffi," he said. "I'm not asking for much, a wife and kids. If you don't love me, maybe over time you'll grow to love me."

She looked him straight in the eyes and said, "Do you think that would be fair to you? You deserve to have someone who loves you as much as you love them and not a friend pretending it's love. David, you deserve more than that because you're a terrific person with fantastic attributes. Women die to have intelligent, good-looking, successful, responsible men who love kids and have everything going for themselves, a home, nice car, and a good job." He had passed for Esther's father many times without trouble. Vanessa's kids were human replica to him, and maybe that's why he clung to them. She reached over, touched his face with her hand, and said, "Why do you want to bog yourself down with a woman with four children and none belonging to you? You're good people, but there's no love connection for either one of us. We're just friends, and that's not fair to you."

"I love your children, and you know I do. If you want to wait a year or two, I'll wait until you're ready."

"Tonight, I'll give you my answer," she said with a wink. "But I'm not going to promise you a thing, so don't get your hopes up too high."

He respected her wish and left so that she could sort through her decision. As she thought about the question, she realized it wasn't the same as when Donald sung his proposal to her, which had caused chills to run down her spine. She had been in love with Donald, and she had had peace about the whole ordeal. She had no feelings for David, and that bothered her. And she felt it would be a disaster for them both to pursue a marriage out of pure convenience.

While she sat on the sofa, sunk down, looking for strength she said, *Dear God, I've been asked a serious question and I need to know what to do. Should I marry David? I'll marry if it's in your will. Should I wait Lord? This is a major decision that shouldn't be taken carefree. I believe in the unity of marriage and the vows that come with it. I need you to direct me.*

Looking up at the ceiling for strength, uneasiness began to creep upon her entire being as she thought about marriage to David. The Holy Spirit was consuming her with feelings of apprehension. But she tried to convince herself that she was doing the wrong thing by not marrying him because of his goodness and kindheartedness. In her mind, she wanted to override the Holy Spirit.

When the kids woke up, she headed to her mom's house. Taffi had called her prior to leaving and asked her to go out for coffee because she needed to talk to get stuff off her mind. Paul Thomas was home and said he would baby-sit.

They decided to go into the same coffee shop where Paul Thomas proposed to Kate, and Donald to Taffi. The shop was the hottest to have good, long, uninterrupted conversations. They wanted to go for their walk, but, instead, went to the coffee shop because it was too cold outside. The shop had never changed. It was busy. The smells of brewing coffee and ham and sausage saturated the place. The sounds of people talking and pots and pans banging filled the air. The waiter took their order, and Taffi said, "Mom, David has asked me to marry him."

"David. Who is David?" Kate asked as she listened.

"I'm sorry. Sgt. Perry told me to call him David."

The waiter returned with their coffee, and Taffi reached for the sugar and said, "But I don't love him. He's a friend, and, a real sweetheart. He feels that love will come later in the relationship. Mom, Donald, and I loved each other before the engagement. How did you feel when you and dad got engaged?"

Kate answered, "When I first met your father in the parking lot, it was love at first sight. I knew he was the one for me. He knew I was the one for him. When he disappeared, my heart was broken. I couldn't eat or sleep and I didn't want to be in the presence of other people. All I wanted was to find him because I was lost without him. Once I found him again and looked into his eyes, the feeling we had, boy, was love. We embraced for a long time drenched in tears of joy, love, and compassion for one another. I didn't want to ever let him go," Kate, said through tears from the ecstasy that the recollection gave her. She studied Taffi over the rim of her coffee cup, "And today, I still feel the same way toward your father. I love him."

"That's how I felt with Donald, but I don't feel this way with David. I told him I would give him an answer tonight. I hate hurting his feelings. He had been good to the kids and me. Someday, maybe I'll grow to love him."

"Sometimes hasty decisions are made, or, in your case, you have consulted God, but you don't want to listen to His answer. Don't go along with your mind or your emotions. Go with what comes from your heart. Let's pray, acknowledge Him and ask Him to direct your path." She took Taffi's hand and prayed, *Dear heavenly Father, we come to you in need of an answer to a question posed to Taffi today. You know her destiny, her future. Should she marry David or wait? We love, You, Lord and turn this whole situation over to You.*

Taffi sat with her eyes shut. She heard a small, still voice, the same she had heard earlier, say, "*Wait!*" Straight away, her eyes opened and she said, "I must wait."

"Okay, that's your answer," said Kate. "I'll never override what the Holy Spirit said to you, and, likewise, you should be obedient to Him also. I don't know your destiny or what the Lord has in store for you. I'm to serve the Lord, not take His place with answers," she said. "There's no compromising on your part, no matter how much you want to have it your way or hate hurting David feelings. If you decide to go against the Holy Spirit, be ready to suffer the consequences. We have choices to make, but it's up to us to make the right choices. Follow the Lord and you won't go wrong."

Taffi, He has something better in store. Don't blow it because of your stubbornness."

Taffi loved and respected her mother. Her wisdom and knowledge was remarkable.

Taffi had a flushed face. "Mom, how am I going to tell David without hurting his feelings? He's a good friend, and I hate losing his friendship. We've been through a lot together, and, as you know, he has been with me every step of the way, helping me with the kids.

Kate's outlook tugged at Taffi's heart, and she said, "Mom, you're right. It's up to me to do the right thing."

Kate studied her, "The Holy Spirit will tell you what you ought to say when the time comes; therefore, have faith, daughter. For the rest of the afternoon, your father and I will watch the kids to allow you time alone. Is that a deal?"

She peeped over the rim of her coffee cup and said, "Thanks, mom."

A joy came over Taffi as she walked into her house. She was taking steps of obedience and looked forward to what God was about to do in her life. She hurried and got the kids clothes and Esther's medication together and took it over to her mom's house. She felt that the Lord was going to crown her efforts with victory.

She went back home to prepare for the night. As she meditated, the enemy tried to step into her thoughts and lead her to go against the Holy Spirit. Since her strength was powerless, she sought the face of God. After confronting Him, she got back on track and knew what she needed to do.

She was sitting in her living room, drinking a cup of tea, at 5:30 P.M. when the doorbell rang. Looking out the peephole, she saw that it was Steven and not David. She knew he hadn't missed a day of visiting his children since he got out of prison. His visit was not a complete surprise. But she didn't want to be bothered right then.

She neatened her hair and opened the door. He noticed that she was awkward as she gazed at him from the opened door and didn't invite him inside. He was dressed nice in a yellow and navy blue polo shirt with navy slacks. Even the casual clothing he wore looked sophisticated on him. The shirt he was wearing magnified his amazing hazel colored eyes. She said forthright, "Steven, I'm sorry, but the kids are staying over my mom's tonight if you want to visit them there."

He answered with a question, "Are you going to invite me inside?"

She allowed him to come in and confessed, "I'm having company over in bit."

He narrowed his eye at her, "Taffi, I have been thinking, long and hard, you have been a charm to take my kids in when they had no other place to go. With all that on your plate now, with Esther's sickness, I thought that if my kid's came to stay with me, things would be better for you."

She made a face at him, "Where did you get a genius idea? Vanessa gave me custody of her kids, and I'll uphold my promise to her and keep them. They are my children now."

He looked at her carefully and said, "I've spoken with a lawyer, and he told me if I go to court it's a possibility that I'll get my children back. I don't want to hurt you since you've been a wonderful mother. But now you need to focus more on the needs of your daughter. And not be burdened with three additional kids that aren't yours."

She inhaled a deep breath, "Who are you to tell me what I need to focus on and what I'm burdened with? You, of all people, can't say a word to me. I helped you when no one else would and allowed you to see your kids because every child needs a father if they have one. I have been crazy to allow you to reappear into their lives again. I felt sorry for you, and this is how you repay me by taking me to court for custody? I had forgiven you of your past, as Vanessa had told me to tell you that she had forgiven you. And look what you're all about, nothing but hurt and pain."

He snapped at her, "What?" Why didn't you ever tell me that Vanessa forgave me? Why did you hold that back from me?"

She snapped right back at him, "I held back because I thought you wouldn't care about her forgiveness, or maybe I thought deep down that you didn't deserve forgiveness, despite how much you've changed."

He shook his head. "Taffi, you've been holding this anger inside for a long time toward me. You can't forgive me or look beyond the past. You can't see that I'm trying to be a good father to my children, can you? Do you think this is all an act?"

She dropped her cup on the end table, "No, yes, whatever! I'm not going to answer your questions. I think you're using me as you used Vanessa. Everything is all about Steven. Nothing has changed."

She blew out a frustrated breath and said, "Did you know she had lost her job? To top that off, she was almost homeless. Vanessa and the three children you cared so much about were thrown out in the streets with nowhere to go because you were too immature to uphold your masculine obligations. It's no wonder she pitched in the towel on life."

He shook his head and said, "I never thought that you were insensitive and heartless, Taffi. I put you on a higher pedestal than what you are showing me now. I have been eaten up inside because she is dead, and I can't ever say I'm sorry to her. In addition, I was guilty wondering had I not been there that night would she have lived. You withheld pertinent information from me, plus you, of all people, are digging up my past, but I've changed."

He frowned, disappointed at her, and asked, "Didn't you think that would be important to me? We have been around each other for months. Don't you know me? I know everything about you," he said, looking down at her with tears in his eyes. "Do you have a heart or any feelings for others?"

She listened to him as the tears entered her tear ducts. Unable to move from her position, she sat immobilized. She squeezed her eyes shut and started to cry. "What went wrong?" she asked.

Disapproving, he said, with an unbearably hurt facial expression, "Don't you care to know me as an individual? I have changed, Taffi. I'm responsible. I'm caring. Do you even care about me at all?" he demanded to know.

Shouting over his calm voice she said, "Yes, I care. Well, I did care, up until today." Tears continued to flow down her cheeks. "Why would you want to take your kids away from me when I promised Vanessa I would care for them? I want you to go, right now," she said as she opened her door.

He exited the front door, "I'm gone, but believe me, this isn't the end of this talk. Tomorrow you'll hear from my lawyer," he said and inhaled a deep breath.

She slammed the door behind him, strode to her bedroom, threw her body across the bed, and cried. The last time anyone talked to her with force was Kate when she wouldn't take up her responsibility as a parent after Esther's birth. Taffi had never had a male friend talk to her the way he had spoken to her. *Lord, I don't deserve this bitterness from Steven. Father, don't let him take Vanessa's kid away.* She cried some more.

Around 7:30 P.M., she heard a knock, and she had forgotten that David was coming over. She got off the bed, ran into the bathroom, and in the mirror she saw a horrible face that was flooded with tears. She ran her hand through her matted hair, took a washcloth and wiped her face, and straightened her wrinkled clothes. She didn't want to answer the door because she was in no condition to talk. She heard another knock. This time it was so much louder that she yelled with all the strength she gathered, "I'll be right there."

She answered the door, and David was disturbed when he saw her appearance.

He asked, "What is going on? Why are you crying?"

She told him about the conversation she had with Steven. He asked, "Did he put his hand on you?"

She threw an alarming stare at him. Without hesitation, she took up for Steven and said, "No, he has changed." She was positive of what she was saying. She didn't understand where that remark came from because she was fuming at Steven and wanted no part of him.

He rubbed his forehead hard, "What will make this better for you? Do you want me to stay or go?" he asked innocently.

She said, "Stay here until I tell you the answer to your question you asked me earlier today. I have sought the Lord, and I feel that He wants me to wait. God is shutting this door, but when the time is right, He'll open another door for you. I'm sorry if this hurts, but I'm going to be obedient. I love you, but as a friend would love a friend. You're always welcomed to visit the kids or me. Let's continue to be friends," she said.

He held her hand, "Are you sure that's your final answer?"

She nodded and said, "I'm sorry."

He hesitated a moment and said, "A blind man is capable of seeing what's going on here."

She added jerking, "What are you talking about? I don't see a thing."

He countered, "I do, because the picture is visible to the eye. Open your eyes and you'll be able to see it as clear as everyone else."

Chapter 11

Steven strolled to his car and called Paul Thomas on his cellular phone. When he spoke to him, Paul Thomas said that he was available to speak since the house was quiet. Kate had taken the kids to the movies and wasn't returning until around 8:30 P.M. Paul Thomas was his boss and a magnificent mentor. He felt confident that he would give him a straight answer. Steven, at times, didn't agree with his suggestions, but he would find out the hard way that Paul Thomas was normally right. Steven recalled when he first started working for Paul Thomas, and he suggested that he purchase a bike to get around until he got on his feet and purchased a car. Steven tried it his way first, but was satisfied with the suggestion because it was more feasible. What he liked was Paul Thomas' sincere love for God and his ability to live what he talked.

Steven headed straight over to Paul Thomas's house. He knew that he was a changed man when he didn't respond by going into a tantrum when Taffi assaulted him verbally. By the time he reached Paul Thomas's house, Steven was at peace with the situation and Taffi's outburst.

Paul Thomas escorted him into his living room. "I'm sorry to bother you today, sir, but I spoke with your daughter, and the conversation got heated. I told her that I was trying to gain custody again. Sir, I'm one hundred percent changed for the better in my attitude and my responsibility as a father. I thought it would help her if I took the kids off her hands. She could focus more on Esther, since she requires more medical attention right now. I guess my intent was wrong. Do you understand what I'm trying to do, sir? Am I wrong for caring enough to help her out, make her burdens lighter?" he asked.

Steven tried to meet Paul Thomas's gaze and continued, "She told me about Vanessa and how she failed to convey a message to me that Vanessa had forgiven me. Sir, I wish I could turn back the hands of time and tell Vanessa that I was sorry for all the hurt I caused her. I shouldn't have been at her house that night late. I was young, jealous, and stupid. I didn't kill her, pastor, and that's the truth," he said with tears flowing. "The system found me guilty, but the Lord and I know the truth. I thought Taffi understood and wouldn't pass judgment, but I see that I was wrong. From the first time I saw your daughter, I loved her, and I love her still, despite all that she has said to me. I always thought, because of my past, I was beneath her, yet I've suppressed my feelings toward her. But now. . ." Steven closed his eyes at the remark. "When she answered the door the day I first visited the kids, I knew that I loved her. Pastor, I have made a lot of mistakes or wrong decisions in my life, but my heart is changed. I'm a new creature. Why can't she see that in me, sir?" he asked.

Paul Thomas replied, "Son, don't worry what others think of you, and never let them determine your value or your worth. God sees your full potential and that's what counts. What's important is that you're somebody special in the eyes of the Lord, not in others eyes. You're His child, and He keeps no record of your mistakes after you've repented. He sees your changed heart toward your children and toward life. People are different. They keep records," he said. "What do you want to do? Do you want me to go over with you while you talk to her?"

Steven shrugged, "That would be a blessing to have an impartial person in on the conversation."

Paul Thomas called Taffi to make sure that she was there. He didn't tell her that he was bringing a guest. Within five minutes, they arrived.

Taffi was still sitting on the sofa when she heard a thump on the door. She didn't peep through the peephole because Paul

Thomas called her. She opened the door and was shocked to see Steven behind her dad. She looked at Steven with disapproval.

Taffi took a seat next to her father, and Steven sat on the love seat across from them. Steven led the conversation. He said with politeness "Taffi, I feel it was unfair how you came down on me today. I was doing what I thought was right to help you out. You have many issues in your life, and if I took three of those away, you'd be better off. I was thinking about you," he admitted with an innocent face.

She began, "I didn't feel that sense of sympathy that you were having for me. I felt deceived and trapped by you. Steven, can't you see that your children are happy here. I love each one of them as I do my own child. For you to think about taking them from this secure environment is selfish and immature. I'll never forgive you for even thinking about taking me to court," she tried to meet his eyes. "That is not right, Steven."

Paul Thomas interjected, "Taffi, this is the first time I've ever brought this up since it happened, and now I do it only to demonstrate a point, then never again. We all have fallen short of the glory of God. Look back. Do you remember when you didn't take up your responsibility as a mother after you had Esther, and God forgave you? Now, if God forgave you your trespasses, why can't you forgive others theirs? There's not one perfect person in this room or in this world. The perfect person died over 2000 years ago to allow us life. You have to work out your problems, not cower from them. We're warriors on the battlefield for the Lord. We battle to do what's right."

She listened and said with power, "Okay, father, I get the point loud and clear."

"Steven, I said some things I should've kept to myself. I felt hurt, and I attacked back with hurting words about your wife and you. Please forgive me for how I over-reacted," she said.

Steven studied her every move and said, "No, Taffi, do you forgive me is the question." He gallantly marched over to her side and placed his hand on her shoulder. He held her hand as she began to nibble on her lower lip. When he touched her, a chill went crawling up her spine. She remembered the conversation that she and Kate had about feelings, and she was experiencing it right now as Steven touched her hand. His hand was gentle and soft, yet powerful. She felt the security of his hand in hers. It was hard for her to focus because he was staring into her eyes. He was handsome and childlike, yet mature and gentle. She had to forgive him. As she looked at him, she was melting inside and withdrew her hand as she glimpsed at her father because her feelings for Steven were getting eerie.

Steven shook his head as he touched her face softly, "I should have taken a better approach than to threaten you with court. Those were fighting words. Moreover I wanted your attention to understand I . . ." he pointed his finger at her, "I care about you," he said and inhaled a deep breath. She was stunned at the words he uttered.

His tone tugged at her heart, "I wanted you to have the best because with a heart such as yours, you deserve more than to be stuck raising three extra children when I'm their biological father, and your child needs you. The burden should be on me and not you. You are an innocent bystander stuck in a drift. A drift produced by me, because I lacked the realization of what a real family is all about."

She shut her eyes and with discretion said, "This drift I chose to endure because nothing happens in life without purpose."

Paul Thomas saw that he needed to exit, so he excused himself at once and said, "You two work this out."

As he walked out of the room, neither one noticed. Steven said, "There's no way I intended to hurt you because I love you." As he talked, she was melting away as she beamed into his eyes.

"You've hurt me, and I've hurt you too. I'm sorry," she said with tears flowing steady from her cheeks.

He reached over with his fingers, and he wiped the tears off her face. He kissed her crimson colored cheeks, and she didn't resist. "I love you, Taffi, and I would love it if you would marry me and be my helpmate for life."

She inhaled a deep breath. "Are you serious?" she asked.

He dropped his hand down by his side, "Yes, I'm serious. As I told your father tonight in the car, I fell in love with you the first time my eyes saw you. I have matured and am ready to be the husband and the father that God required me to be. He has given me a second chance, and I won't blow it this time around. I promise to fulfill my obligations as a husband and a father," he said and grinned.

She took a step backward and said, "I have to go to the restroom." She spun around toward the bathroom. He was shocked at her response.

In the bathroom, she rested on the closed door. Thrilled she managed to say, *Lord, I come to you again with a long-term decision that I have. Should I marry Steven? I feel it's right to marry him, but I need to hear from you.* She felt a peace come over her that surpassed all her understanding. She knew Steven was the one that God wanted her to marry. *God, earlier, I felt I should wait, and I heeded the warning.* She chuckled and said, *Lord, You had an invisible ram in the brush. I didn't see him coming until today. I was blinded by the brush of everyday living, children, situations, working. . . .* She was breathless as she continued to hold her hand to her heart. Her heart seemed as though it was going to jump out of her chest. She thought *I have to calm down.*

She returned to the living room once she was composed. She watched him sitting, comfortably, on the sofa, and drinking a soda. Her heart was still pounding. Her heart was reacting the same way it had when Donald popped the question. As she sat next to Steven, he straightened, sipped, and tried to appear natural. She murmured against his ear, "I have good news to tell you. I confronted the Lord about marrying you, and I feel at peace. My answer to your question is yes, I'll marry you," she managed to say with a smile along with tears.

He placed his soda down abruptly, yet he gently reached to hug her. He said, "I promise you have not made a mistake. I'll be the husband you imagined me to be and more."

She said with humility, "There's something I think you need to know. Today, David proposed to me also, and I told him no. Steven, I hate hurting his feelings. He's a good friend to the children, to you and to me. David had said some words to me that generated curiosity in me. It was as though he knew about my feelings for you even before I knew them. I was clueless to his observation."

He sighed and said, "I think we both sensed a yearning for each other, yet we were both stubborn. Back to your question, I feel it's right to tell him our plan to marry and to get his blessings. Don't you, Taffi?"

"I'll invite him over for breakfast tomorrow morning," she said.

They decided to marry in one month. All the children would be in the wedding party. Her father would marry them at Pine Outreach Center. After making those plans, Taffi changed the subject.

"I've been thinking, Steven, you've gone through a lot in your life, and I need to learn to forget your past and look to our future together. Your first marriage had issues that I feel need discussing before we take this relationship to another level. Let's compile a list of issues to talk over to bring everything to light and get all differences reconciled to make certain our lives together will be successful. I want no darkness to prevail over the marriage." She went and got paper and pencil and they begin working.

Following considerable exploration of the concern areas, Taffi started the discussion, "Steven, when we fight, let's do it decently and in order, without causing pain to one another. Wrong words destroy; therefore, let's say the right words to one another.

He said, "And we won't judge each other because it is hurtful, and horrible results occur." She said, "From this day forward, I won't judge your past or your actions from the past. We'll be open and compassionate to one another's needs."

He added, "I think it's important that you know the truth. I didn't kill Vanessa. I was gone and whatever happened to her happened. I want it clear before we get married in order that there is never be any doubt in your mind of my innocence. I'll never hurt you," he reiterated.

She approved with a smile. "No doubt in my mind that you are telling the truth," she announced.

She shook her head, "Let's get rid of any anger in our hearts before we confront one another on any issues. Hurt occurs when needs aren't met by all parties; therefore, let's meet each other's needs. I've found that the best way to do that is to communicate feelings and talk it out as we are now. Let's learn to talk to one another."

She was about to say more when he stopped her by placing his finger over her mouth. He whispered in her ear, "My communication skills are super," and he kissed her lips.

She said breathlessly, "I'm going to go to the next point." She flapped her hand and hit him teasing, "You're being bad."

He watched her with approval, "I know, but the results I'm getting from you are worth it."

She said, "Let's avoid laziness in our marriage and be willing to help each other out. We have four children, and all the work shouldn't be put on anyone person. I feel we won't have a problem with this issue because you're helping me out now," she pointed out. "Don't change what you're doing, Steven."

She studied him and continued, "I'm a believer that a family that prays together stays together. Let's make prayer an everyday occurrence in our household."

She retreated with a bashful appearance, "I hate talking about my first husband because it can offend you, and I don't want you to live up to his behavior. I'll never judge you against him, and I hope you do the same. He satisfied me; therefore, I want you to know what he did for me. He always complimented me. We went on dates. He wrote me special love notes. He gave me gifts. We spent valuable time together. We were best friends and lovers. And he was intimate, yet it wasn't all about him, but about serving me. I was the queen, and he was the king."

He hesitated a moment, and said, "I see I've some hard shoes to fill, and I'm willing to fill them. I'll never be Donald, even though I do some of the positive things you spoke of because I was that person to my numerous girlfriends."

She tried again, "Don't get me wrong, I'm not asking you to fill Donald's shoes, and I'm not trying to fill Vanessa's shoes. It's hard enough filling our own shoes. All I want you to do is to think first before you make choices concerning our relationship and family. The main thing is showing forgiveness and understanding one another."

He thought long and hard about what to say. As he started talking, he held her hand. He was restless as he sat next to her on the sofa. Her presence in his life rejuvenated his body, soul, and mind. "Taffi..." he began, "I've always been the type person who loved myself and wasn't ashamed to show my self-centeredness. I pampered my faults and failures, instead of changing them. Let me tell you about the new and revised Steven Hawkins. He's learning the Word and knows what Christ demands of him. I'll be everything you imagined a husband to be and more. I have learned during my growing up stages that I'm ready to settle down. Months before I asked you to marry me, I knew you were the one for me. I asked God what to do to win you over. He exposed that I needed to change first by putting Him first in my life. God revealed everything that you've spoken about today. I'll obey your every wish. I love you, Taffi, and I want the best for you," he said and touched her brightened face. "I want to spend the rest of my life with you, pleasing you every minute of the day. I've learned a lot in prison. First, life is short, and you have to make the best of it before it passes you by. Second, choose your true friends carefully, the ones that'll stick by you through thick and thin. Family will stick around. You were a friend to me first without knowing me. You showed me light through your kindness in a dark, dreary place. The basic letters you sent me shined bright on my dull life. I've seen how you're a good mother and a good person to others. You didn't think I was paying close attention to you. I couldn't help enjoy how you smile, how you nibble on your lower lip when you are thinking, and how you flip your left hand up when you're frustrated. You're biting your lower lip now. Look at you! I've said a lot, but you've nothing to worry with because I've got it together now."

After he made the comment about her lip, she dropped her hand from his powerful grip as if she had touched a hot burner. She said, "I never noticed that I nibbled on my lip before today. It must be a nervous reflex," she said and placed her hand on her mouth.

Steven always noticed Taffi's every move whenever he visited or was in her presence. Even as he played with the kids, he was spotting her every action. Many of her actions had touched him, but the one that touched him most was this past summer when he had taken the kids to the park and Taffi tagged along. An elderly woman was sitting alone on the park bench, watching as the children played. Taffi directed Esther to pick one of the flowers in the flowerbed and offer the flower to the woman. She instructed Esther and Jasmine that they are to touch other people's lives through acts of kindness. Esther took Jasmine by the hand, and they did as Taffi instructed, and it brightened the woman's life. Today, he had to let her know how she influenced his life. His voice intensified as he spoke, "I have noticed the simple things you do to brighten lives, and that distinguishes you from other women I've met."

She responded, "Is that supposed to make me feel better? I'm honored to know that I rank above your rating for other women, since I'm about to marry you in a month."

"Come on now, none of that nonsense." He cleared his throat, "Let me pick up where I left off. Imprisonment opened my eyes to my faults because I was able to look at the real me. I was able to recognize where I went wrong. I found the following areas to be my shortcomings: trust, letting go of stuff, making my marriage work and speaking positive words. You see, I've learned that marriage requires commitment every second of the day. I failed at marriage the first time, and, this time around, I want to get it right. I'll do what is required of me every second of the day. And our marriage will be okay."

She pointed out, "I'm willing to make this marriage work, too."

To escape what he was feeling, he looked at the snow as it began to trickle to the ground. He dropped the tissue out his hand and tried to stay focused on outside. Glaring out the window, he focused on a large, barking, dog scurrying across the street with a small child following behind him. It was obvious that the dog was no match for the unsupervised child. Picking the tissue up he said, "Taffi... I love you."

"I guess, I had seen things about you that I liked also," she said without hesitation. She couldn't bring herself to say that she loved him. When Donald died, she decided in her mind that she would never love a man the way that she loved him because it would be too hurtful if something happened to him.

They talked for a couple more hours into the twilight until both were exhausted. With a smile, she managed to say, "Let's call it quits, Steven, or we'll be here all night."

"There's one more concern I want to address. This topic is touchy because many people have different views of cohabitation and sex outside of marriage. I'm not a virgin anymore because I've been married before and have a child, but I do obey the no cohabiting and no sex before marriage requirement that the Lord has ordained. I also conformed to these same rules with Donald as well." She looked at him, "Tonight, you'll have to go home. We'll be married in one month, and, at that time, we'll follow all the rules of marriage. I don't mean to be harsh, but I have to do the right thing in order to live with myself and please God. Are we on the same sheet of music?"

"Yes, we're on the same sheet of music," he said. "I'll live with the rules you're enforcing." Part of him wanted to do right, and the other part didn't care about sinning. He said, "I'm a new believer, but I want to do the right versus wrong. I'll go home. I appreciate your honesty and purity because I have gone out with many church-going females, and they were different because they allowed me to stay over and to have sex with them. Taffi, I'm glad you stand for righteousness. He gathered his coat, disappointed, yet relieved that the enemy hadn't won. For the first time in his lifetime, a female had turned him down, and that wounded his carnal ego. He shrugged his shoulders as he tightened the coat to shield the cold out. *She should have at least offered me the couch to sleep on, being it's snowing outside,* he thought.

After he left, Taffi reflected on her day, and, overall, she said it was a good day. She never thought she would marry again, but God knew. She couldn't wait to call Kate and let her in on the good news. They had work ahead of them to get everything planned in a short period.

She hoped her dealing with the death of Donald would usher in triumph when she married Steven. But somehow, she knew differently. She was elated that life turned into a direction she never predicted.

The next morning, Taffi got up early, despite her late night of planning and talking with Steven. She never imagined she would be marrying Steven. If she had a choice to pick a partner between Steven and David, she would have picked David over Steven because his records were cleaner. God created the heaven and the earth, and she would never question why he picked Steven over David. But He opened the doors and allowed Steven inside. The God she served had devised a plan, and no one could destroy the plan He devised. She was elated because she was marrying the biological father of the children she was raising as her own. Who was she to dispute destiny?

She called her parents, and her father answered the phone. "Father, I have some shocking, yet exciting news to tell you. Steven has asked me to marry him."

"Congratulations, daughter. Steven informed me of his plans yesterday." Paul Thomas remembered that he sensed that Steven wanted to say something more as they sat silent in the car in the driveway of Taffi's residence. As he spoke his intentions, Paul Thomas was happy for him, and he gave Steven his blessings. He told him about when he and Kate first met, it was love at first sight, and he knew she was the one chosen for him. He even recounted how he was down and out, and she still was there for him. Paul Thomas liked Steven and thought he was a wonderful man that had had bad circumstances in his life.

Paul Thomas handed Kate the phone after he finished passing on good wishes. When Taffi told Kate what was going on, she asked her if she had confronted the Lord first before making her decision. Once she heard her answer, she was happy. She reported the plans thus far, and, of course, Kate added more.

After talking with Kate, Taffi knew her next step was to confront David. She picked up the phone and dialed his number. She closed her eyes at hearing him, "David, this morning before you go to work, please stop by because I need to talk to you." He told her he would be over within the next thirty minutes. She called Steven and told him to come right over.

She had thought about what she was going to say and had devised an approach that she thought would be successful. Both men showed up around the same time. She escorted them into the living room. She had wanted the atmosphere to be right, so she lit the fireplace and let it heat the room before they came over. She had placed a pot of coffee on the coffee table, and she poured them each a cup. She reached for her cup and began to circle her finger around the rim. "Friendship means a lot to me, and all three of us have become good friends. Steven, you asked me yesterday to marry you, and, by the Lord's leading, I told you no. Before we were born, the Lord knew every hair on our heads, and everyone has a destiny. He knew I would fall in love with Donald, marry him, and have precious Esther. He had named her before her birth. He knew that Vanessa would be in my life, and that shortly thereafter, she'd die and turn over her children to me, a single mom. He also knew what I'm about to tell you would happen. David has asked me to marry him. It is ironic that it happened on the same day. Deep down, I felt a peace versus the discomfort I felt with you. I'm sorry, David. Nonetheless, I feel that the Lord wants me to marry Steven. It's my and Steven's destiny, and yours is yet to come."

She took a sip and tried to look normal as she studied David's motions. At first, she didn't think he was taking it well. He turned his face away, but regained his composure. She hated having this conversation, but knew no other way, except in person. She continued, "David, I don't want you to hate or despise either one of us. That's why we're having this conversation. We don't want any hard feelings between us. We love you as the friend you are, and want to continue our relationship. We aren't out to make enemies or to hurt you in any way. May we have your blessing, along with your continued friendship?"

He shrugged a shoulder, shed tears, looked down, and then raised his head and said, "That's touching. The way you let me down. I never want to stop our friendship. You thought enough of me to get my blessings. I have grown to love you all, including the kids, as a family. Taffi and Steven, you have my blessings under one condition."

They both looked at one another and glared at him and said, "What is it David?" Taffi asked.

He said, "That I be allowed to be the best man." He chuckled as he poured himself another cup of coffee. David said, "Yesterday, Taffi, when you spoke about Steven, I knew you were in love with him. I'm happy for you both, and I have no animosity. You're right, Taffi. One day I'll find my destiny.

"Deal," they all shouted, and they gave each other a hug.

The next step was to tell the children. They decided to do it at her parents house. Taffi called Kate and told her the plans, and she told them not to come until after naptime.

At about two-thirty, they showed up. They were full of love and admiration for one another. Kate observed that her daughter was happy again. Love was so fulfilling and significant that she quoted 1 John 4:7, 10. *Dear friends, let us love one another, for love comes from God. Everyone who loves is born of God, and knows Him. Whoever doesn't love doesn't know God, because God is love. This is how God showed his love among us: he sent his one and only Son into the world that we might live through him. This is love: not that we loved God, but that he loved us and sent his Son as an atoning sacrifice for our sins.* Kate related to love because she had been in love with Paul Thomas for close to forty years, and their love never swayed.

Kate gave the kids a snack once they awakened and told them to meet her in the living room when they finished. Taffi,

Paul Thomas, Kate, and Steven were having a conversation when the children entered the room.

Esther started to ramble to Taffi about all the fun they had had at grandma's house and Jasmine interposed. The conversation settled down enough to speak. "Children, your mom has some good news to tell you. Let her have your undivided attention."

Jackie asked mystified, "Grandma, what is undivided?"

Kate looked at her and chuckled, "Honey, it means not to look or play around, but listen carefully to what is said."

"Okay, grandma." They all approved and started to watch Taffi closely. She was even more nervous talking with the children than in her talk with David, and she didn't know why. She didn't know if this was going to confuse them. The last thing she wanted was to get a mess started.

Taffi had thought hard about how she would conduct the conversation with her kids, and Kate had taken some of the burden off her. When she turned to Esther, Jasmine and Jackie seated in front of her, she said, "This is a story about a woman at the well. A woman one day walked slowly because life was weighing her down. She wasn't old, but she seemed old by how she acted. She had made some bad choices that left her heart empty and hopeless. The sad woman had not felt loved for a long time. She thought she'd never be able to love again. The woman was carrying a water bucket on her head at the well alone. She saw a man resting on the well. She thought he was a Jew, and during those times, Jews thought they were better than Samaritans were. She wanted to stay away from him. She went around the well and lowered her bucket into the water. The man asked her to give him a drink of fresh cool water. She told him that she couldn't believe he was speaking to her, a Samaritan. She acted tough. She didn't know the man was Jesus. As they talked, Jesus showed her he knew many things about her life. She was uncomfortable and wanted to run away. As she listened to him, the crust around her heart began to melt. 'God loves you,' Jesus said. 'He wants your worship.' She said, 'He can't love me. I've done many bad things.' She said she couldn't understand the talk about God, and she heard that the Messiah was coming. Jesus looked the woman and said, 'I'm the Messiah!' The woman ran back to town shouting, 'I met the Messiah. Come with me. I want you to meet him too!'"

Taffi took a breather and asked, "When the woman at the well met Jesus, what did she do?"

Jasmine answered, "She went to the town shouting."

Paul Thomas said, "Yes, she wanted everyone to have the same experience she had."

Taffi continued, "When you have wonderful news, what's the first thing you want to do?"

Esther answered, "I want to tell someone."

Taffi looked at Steven and said, "Your father and I have some exciting news to share today with you all. We're getting married."

Jackie asked, "What is getting married?"

Steven looked at her and said, "It's when two people, a man and a woman, say vows in front of God, themselves and friends to join them together as one, husband and wife."

Esther shouted, "It's similar to grandpa and grandma. They live together, do things together, and they sleep together in the same house."

Jasmine said, "It's having a mommy and a daddy. Right now, we have a mommy. Our mom that went to heaven always said we didn't have a father. Will you Mommy J cry, like my other mom?"

Steven glanced down at her and said, "That daddy is gone forever, I have grown up."

Taffi answered, "How do you feel about hearing the good news?"

They answered and said one at a time, "All right."

Chapter 12

Looking up at the cloudy sky from the window, Taffi knew it was going to be a rainy day. Nevertheless, it didn't bother her because her life was in no way near dreary, but instead full of excitement. In one week, she would be tying the knot. Three weeks had passed since she said yes to Steven, and the time had flown by fast. Everyday she was busy planning or doing something related to the wedding. Grandma Betty was coming to town, and that was always a thrill. She was coming to help with the wedding.

They were meeting at the coffee shop for breakfast at ten o'clock. Taffi had taken a three-week vacation, one week each for the wedding, honeymoon, and adjusting. She had arranged the breakfast to tell her grandmother of all the details of the wedding.

At breakfast, her grandmother suggested that she wanted to walk down the aisle since she never had during her lifetime. Because Grandma Betty had suggested a bizarre request, Taffi was willing to conform without reservation.

Betty was unusual for an eighty-three-year old. She acted as if she was in her fifties, and she looked young, too. The aging process had slowed, and she claimed it was because of her Indian heritage. Betty was still a size eight, wore glasses, and sported a short haircut. People still mistook Kate and Betty to be sisters. It was amazing how Betty got around. She was limber and had a steady pace that was excellent for her age. Betty's primary transportation was by limousine since she stopped driving a year ago.

She loved visiting Kate, but, more than anything, she loved being with her great grandchildren because they brought back her youth. Betty favored Jasmine because reminded her of herself, and she saw she had a jab for business. Although Jasmine was young, she was wise for her age. Betty thought about turning the business over to her one day.

After breakfast, they all headed to Kate's house. Within fifteen minutes of their arrival, loud knocks where heard at the front door. When Betty heard the bang, she darted past Kate and opened the door. Staring out the doorway, she inspected the two extra large bunches of red roses in crystal vases hidden in front of a mysterious person. Within seconds, a delivery boy, wearing earphones, listening to a CD player and moving to whatever music he was listening to, acknowledged her presence when he said, "Delivery for Betty Campbell." She grasped both the vases and sniffed a lungful of the sweet fragrances emitting from the fresh blooming roses. With a smile, she took the roses from the delivery boy.

Inside the house, she placed the vases on the sofa table across from the front door and read the hand-written note, "Betty, let's talk, today!" After arranging the vases on the nearest least occupied table, she returned to the opened door, and swung it almost shut when a hand blocked it from closing. She peered outside, and it was Willie Johnson.

Willie had worked for her company for over fifty years. He was wearing the multicolor motorcycle designed tie she had given him for Christmas. She had gone into a motorcycle specialty store and found the pricey tie because he was fond of motorcycles, and she wanted to please him. Willie was still in good shape for his age. He golfed whenever the weather was nice, and he still was able to work full time. He continued to work in hopes that one day Betty would change her offense on the subject of men and detect that he loved her a good deal. He had tried to convey his love for her many times throughout the years. This was the first time he felt safe to pursue a relationship.

He was Caucasian and stood about 5'6" tall. His entire head was gray, and his eyes were green. At one time, he was a redhead, and a few red strands were still present. He was handsome. He had business savvy and was the reason for her restaurants expansion into twenty states with more still to come. The statement opposites attract was real in their lives. Betty was book smart, private, and successful, whereas he was street smart, sociable, and he thrived on her support.

Betty said, "Thanks for the roses. They're beautiful. What's the occasion?"

Not taking his eyes off her, he responded without blinking, "You're the occasion."

"What do you mean, Willie?" she asked, rolling her eyes at him.

"I'm getting older as we speak, even though I feel young. I'm not as young as I used to be. I have stuck with you through the good and the bad, never leaving your side, despite wanting to numerous times. I've been a branch on your tree that has persevered through your pruning year after year. I've grown strong dealing with your sour attitude about men, and it has paid off to the point that I want more of you. Nine years ago, I noticed a remarkable change wherein you didn't hate men as much anymore, and one year ago was the break in the iceberg. Your newfound lease on men was subtle, yet evident, and today I believe you love men again."

Betty recalled her life revision. A year ago, she went to Dave's funeral and sent flowers to the funeral home with no hatred at all toward him. She even carried him flowers. The visit was instrumental in healing Betty because she forgave him for all the stuff he did. It was amazing how she allowed bitterness to crack open her heart, but it mended."

Willie commented, staring at Betty, "I hung around all these years for this day to happen when you would open up to me. Yesterday, as I watched you sipping coffee, you asked me to sit, and we held a personal conversation for the first time without talking business. I knew your heart had softened and if I didn't move fast, it would be too late. Will you marry me, Betty Campbell? I want to be your husband."

She looked at him with pride and said, "I'm eighty-three years old and have a few good years left."

"I'm the same age as you, Betty. That's why we need to do this before our time runs out," he said gazing flatteringly into her beautiful hazel-colored eyes again. "What do you say about that idea? Everyone deserves some happiness." He took her hands into his shaky, wrinkled, freckled hands.

Betty responded blushing, "Yes, I will marry you, Mr. Willie Johnson."

Once she uttered those words from her mouth, Kate came from behind the stairway and said, "It's about time you two admit you love one another. Come on in, Willie, and we'll talk about a date." Taffi, who was working in the kitchen, came out and rejoiced, too.

Kate directed them into the living room, holding one on each side of her, and helped them to the sofa. She sat in the recliner across from them and studied them as she said, "I'm happy for you both."

They decided to marry in one month, but Taffi suggested they have a double wedding. After careful consideration, they went along with the double wedding suggestion. Betty said, "I'm not getting any younger, the sooner the better." They went and took care of the marriage license, and everything else was easy since Taffi had invited a lot of the family anyway. Those that she didn't invite by mail got invitations via e-mail.

That night Betty found a beautiful sequined white gown, the same as Taffi's, and it fit perfectly with a full-length veil. Everything else was as easy as making phone calls and changing projected numbers. Taffi had a wedding planner, which made things super easy.

Both Betty and Taffi were getting excited as the days flew by. They had been so busy that they had forgotten the meeting they had scheduled with Paul Thomas on the Wednesday before their wedding date. He reminded them about the missed meeting, and they showed up on Thursday instead. Taffi and Steven met with him first, and then Betty and Willie went in for their counseling. Marriage counseling hadn't changed since Taffi had gone through it with Donald. They discussed valuable information about marriage as well as the expectations of each party.

The next day was the rehearsal and the dinner. Everyone was ecstatic, knowing the wedding would occur the day after the rehearsal dinner. Taffi couldn't keep up with the time because each time she looked at her watch hours were blinking by fast. She handed her watch to her friend Tina to keep up with the time.

When Taffi had married Donald, Tina was in the military, stationed overseas, and wasn't able to come home, but this time she was there for her.

The plans were for Paul Thomas to stand in the center of two silver-flowered cathedral arches along with Kate facing the congregation. The grooms would be in their chosen cathedral arch facing the congregation as they each awaited their brides. Dave would stand with the best men. Tina, Taffi's maid of honor, would march first and stand on the right hand side of Taffi's arch. Jasmine and Esther would grace the aisle runner together to stand along aside Tina. Eric, the ring bearer, and Jackie, the flower girl, would march together as Jackie tossed rose petals onto the runner. Jackie, Esther, and Eric would stand next to Kate. Taffi had decided since this was Betty's first wedding, she would go first and thereafter, Taffi would grace the runner. Both couples would stand under their designated silver-flowered cathedral arch. Betty and Willie would do their vows first. Both couples would have a double ring ceremony.

Taffi and the kids had stayed over at Kate's house after the rehearsal dinner. On the morning of the wedding, everybody was up early. Taffi was more nervous the second time around than the first time. Betty showed no fretfulness. Instead, she stayed calm. It was a busy morning at the beauty parlor. When it was over, they all looked beautiful.

As the children got dressed, things started to go wrong. Jasmine couldn't find her shoes. Esther messed up her girlish hairdo. Jackie got candy on her dress, and Eric cried for a toy that Jackie had taken away from him. The enemy was trying to get in the midst. Taffi shouted, "Get thee behind me, satan. I won't let you destroy what is supposed to be a wonderful day for me." And after that, peace came in the room, and it was calm again.

Kate had the fun part of making sure that each bride was wearing something old, something new, something borrowed and something blue. Both wore old slips, new diamond earrings, and borrowed necklaces. It was special when Kate gave each bride a beautiful diamond bracelet with a sapphire stone in the center.

The wedding was to start at 3:00 P.M., and it started right that instant and not a second later. The ceremony was beautiful and without flaws. They exchanged promises to love and honor one another as long as they lived. It was super delightful when Paul Thomas declared them husbands and wives. As the couples strolled down the runner, the congregation cheered them. They were happy for Betty, marrying for the first time at her age.

The reception was in the church. Betty had one of her local restaurants to cater the food. They ate, socialized, and danced the night away. At around ten P.M., the couples dashed off to their separate honeymoons after tossing their bouquets to the unmarried females. The lucky girl to catch Betty's bouquet was Tina, who got back in the group and caught Taffi's bouquet, as well. Before Taffi left, she said, "You're next in line, Miss Tina!"

The day after the wedding ceremony, Taffi and Steven escaped to a secluded island resort by airplane. The temperature on the island was wonderful compared to the cold weather they had left in Pine, Virginia.

The second day into the honeymoon, Steven was on cloud nine, and his love for Taffi exploded to sizeable heights. Heights that he never thought he would ever reach, but he had, and it was remarkable. He was able to receive love from the woman he loved, which was something that he had never done. He wondered if this was all a camouflage and he'd go back to his old self again, or if he had changed. He desired to be different. Somehow, deep down, he didn't know how to sustain a lasting relationship with a woman. In the bed, as he looked at her sleeping, he ran his fingers through her hair as he remembered the important question, "Do you take Taffi James to be your wife?" For the second time in his life he responded, "I do!" to the question. The words rang in his head as they did the moment he got married the first time. He had done it again. Was he dreaming? The reality was that the words petrified him because it meant commitment. They were husband and wife, united as one, and he didn't know if he was cut out to be a husband, let alone a father. He thought he wanted fatherhood, but was skeptical after Esther's hospitalization. He wondered if this was an after prison craze for added attention. His outlook concerning marriage had changed, despite the wonderful love they had shared together.

Everyday they were on the island was full of passion and oneness, and neither one wanted to go. He told her, "If life stayed like this, it would be fabulous." He knew that soon the honeymoon would be ending. She responded as she packed the suitcases, "Wishful thinking, but today we'll be going home to reality, decisions, bills, work, homework, church and juggling all aspects of marriage plus four kids. I hope that you're ready for change because, ready or not, it's happening regardless."

He put his head down on the pillow while she continued packing the suitcases and mumbled, "I know, I know."

Paul Thomas, Kate, and the children were at the airport early. It gave them time to look at the airplanes take off, and whenever they saw one land, the children shouted, "Mommy!" The newlyweds passed security and were in sight of the kids. When Taffi saw them, she ran to them shouting their names, and they all rushed to greet her. They had missed her so much that they didn't want to let her go as they hugged and kissed her. At last, they broke the tight grip, and Paul Thomas and Kate got their turns to hug.

Three days had passed since their return, and Steven sat in the living room staring at the blackened television screen. He had another week off to fine-tune his new lifestyle. He sat staring, remembering his first marriage and how he felt. He loved Taffi; nevertheless, he was feeling as trapped as he did with Vanessa. He felt it must be something mental that didn't allow him to feel comfortable as a married man. He felt as though he had made a big mistake again, after they returned from the honeymoon. He knew his desire to be a father had changed. It had to be his fictitious expectation of what marriage was all about. He thought that once they married everything would flow as before. The difference was he couldn't go home. He was stuck in a living environment that smothered the breath out of him. Steven questioned his life, and it hadn't changed at all. He wanted fewer responsibilities and more freedom. He contemplated if he should tell Taffi how he was feeling or overlook what he was feeling because it would maybe pass. He decided to keep his feelings a secret.

Chapter 13

Taffi planned a special tea for her friend Tina because of her recent promotion to Chief of Administration at Pine Hospital. She had left early after taking the three kids to school and Eric to childcare, and she headed to the grocery store to pick up the special food trays she had ordered. She was excited to do this for Tina.

Kate had come over around 10:30 A.M. to help her prepare for the tea since she had organized many and knew how to set them up. Kate was a blessing, a magnificent leader, loyal to her call as a mother, and gifted in many ways.

At about 11:45 A.M., the guests started to show up. At that time, Steven decided to give Taffi space for her special tea. At first, he was going to check his e-mails at his job, but decided to go to a local car dealership to check out the new cars. The car lot was crowded because a local radio station was promoting a car give-a-way. When he got there, because of the crowd, he decided not to stay long. As he toured the lot, he noticed a woman dressed in a flashy red dress with matching pumps and a fur wrap. He continued to look at the cars when the flashy female touched him on the shoulder.

She said, "Hi, it's been over two years since I've seen you. Where have you been?"

He stepped back, shocked to see that the well-dressed female was someone he knew. Nikki was one of the females he had once had a relationship with before he went to prison. She looked spectacular in the red slinky dress she was wearing. He had tried to call her numerous times while in prison; however, she would never accept the calls. He had written her several times, and the letters came back unopened. Why was she showing an interest now? He sighed. "Had you opened the letters I sent you or answered the phone calls, maybe you would have found out what had happened to me," he declared.

She corrected him, "No, maybe you should have been more persistent."

"I thought we had it going on, but I guess I was mistaken. I spent more time with you than with my own wife and kids. Remember we were even talking about shacking up? You threw it all down the drain when you disregarded my existence while I was in prison."

"I guess I was mad at you for killing your wife. I saw it in the newspaper, and that was enough for me."

"Do you think I would hurt her or even you? To set the record straight, I didn't kill my wife. They charged me for her death even though I proclaimed my innocence. It was an accident. I was charged with negligence because I touched her arm, which they say caused her to stumble and hit her head once she got in her building."

She countered, "I couldn't deal with your problems because I was having problems of my own."

"It was nice seeing you again, but I've remarried and started over again."

"You, start over, and on the good foot? No way! Because you're insensitive to the needs of women and you're harsh on any relationship. I bet it'll never work, and you'll come crying back to my shoulders."

"Well, you have me all wrong. I've changed my whole outlook on life." He moved, as if to walk away from her, but she put her hand on his shoulder.

"You would never be satisfied with one woman because you'll get bored," she said. "Plus, it's not in your nature. When you need a thrill, here's my cell phone number." She took a piece of paper, wrote down her number, and slipped the number into his topcoat pocket. "You knew what we had before, and the apple doesn't fall far from the tree. Call me anytime. You'll be back for more." She smiled as if she knew a secret.

Shaking his head, he said, "You're wrong. I've changed." He left and went to a coffee shop nearby. He had to clear his head of her because she was bad news. His relationship with her had kept him from committing to his family. Drinking his coffee, he was convinced that she was the woman he should've married instead of Vanessa. Now more than ever, he was confused because prior memories of her popped up. *Have I made a mistake again? Maybe I should have picked door number two, Nikki, instead of picking door number one, my wife. I have to cast down these strongholds, or the enemy will trap me again.*

In the shop, he looked into space as though he had lost his best friend. People were coming and going; yet he saw no one. The waiter had refilled his cup every time it was low. He drank the first cup of coffee and another cup. He took the slip of paper she gave him and rubbed it between his fingers. He thought about his beautiful wife at home and their four children and wondered why he was feeling that he needed to pursue her. The feeling of being unappreciated overtook his emotions.

He took out his cell phone and called her up. He told her he wanted to talk to her. She was at a retail store nearby and told him she would meet him at the coffee shop within five minutes. At the table, she said, "I knew you would get bored, but I didn't feel it to be this soon," she teased. "Didn't you say you just got married?"

"I don't know why I called you. I guess I need you," he said. He lifted his hand and closed his eyes, rubbing his forehead hard.

She was fast to point out, "You need to relax and get your mind straight." She stroked her hand alongside his face, "Let's go to my place?" she said, as she captivated him with her eyes. "It's not far from here."

He nodded, "No, I shouldn't. I don't want to do something that I'll be sorry for later."

She scooted close to him and whispered in his ear, "You won't be sorry. If you didn't want me, you wouldn't have called. Don't you agree?" She nibbled on his ear.

Her inducement, along with her beauty, overtook him and the next thing he knew he was holding her hand and had checked into a hotel a few doors down the street. He thought about how hurt Taffi would be. But for some reason, he couldn't resist Nikki's seducing magnetism. She had numbed his outlook on marriage. He was overwhelmed and had to have her no matter what the consequence.

The enemy had set a trap and mesmerized him into an ambush. He was in the room and had taken off his shirt. As he was about to take off his shoes he looked doubtful at her beautiful image. He felt the spirit within him say, "Don't you do it because you have a beautiful wife a home." He fought the intuition to stop what he was doing. He looked at her, "I can't, I'm sorry. I must go." He ran out the hotel room, putting his clothes back on. He was ashamed because he had fallen into the same trap that he did with his first marriage. He couldn't go home until the tea ended, so he headed to work because he needed to vent his frustrations.

Paul Thomas was at the front desk when he entered the building. He greeted him, "How's the honeymoon going, son?"

He spoke, "Sir, everything is going."

Paul Thomas noticed that something wasn't right with him and intervened, "Son, let's go into my office and talk." Observing him, he looked distant and his coat was buttoned up wrong."

"Yes, sir," he said still mystified by his earlier inappropriate actions with Nikki.

He sat across from Paul Thomas as he talked, "When I first married Kate and came home from my honeymoon, I was wary as to whether I had made the right decision, taking on a deep responsibility of taking care of another person. But I got over that feeling suddenly."

"You know about my awful past, and my question is what if I can't live up to my position as a husband or father? I messed up with Vanessa. What if I mess up with your daughter?" He started to cry as Paul Thomas handed him a tissue. "What if I'm not strong enough to withhold the temptations of other females? What if I should have waited before taking this great responsibility?"

"Son, you have to get rid of the guilt of what you did in your first marriage and attempt to do the opposite of the wrong you did. Yes, you messed up and made mistakes as everybody else makes mistakes and messes up."

"Do they make them after the honeymoon? Let me explain, I love your daughter…"

Paul Thomas interrupted before he said another word, "No, I don't want you to explain to me what happened or didn't happen. Instead, go to the Lord, repent, and talk it over with your wife because that's what's needed. Telling me won't solve a thing. There's not one perfect person on this earth. The only perfect person that walked on earth was Jesus Christ. Pray and ask Him to give you strength because we've all sinned and fallen short of the glory of God. Depend on God because He is faithful if you allow Him to work. Sometimes when you're tempted, you're not looking for a way out; instead, you're looking for a doorway into pleasure. What I'm saying is there's a right and a wrong way of handling temptations. The right way takes the power of resistance, and the wrong way will give you temporary satisfaction. Quote the Word when you need it to work in your life."

"Thank you for listening to me and helping me through this mess." They shook hands, and Steven went into the sanctuary, knelt at the altar, and cried. *"Lord, I love You, and I serve You. I have fallen short of Your glory. I thank you Father for letting me escape the enemy's schemes designed to destroy me. I haven't lived up to the standards You have set for me as a husband. Instead, I have been promiscuous with lust. Lust is sin, and it is as wrong as adultery. My heart was full of lustful desires for Nikki that almost led me to commit adultery. Adultery destroyed my first marriage, and now it's about to destroy my relationship with Taffi. I want to change my dreadful ways. I repent of those sins, and I'm asking You to forgive me of my sins, change my heart, and help me to be committed to my wife. My asking for forgiveness doesn't condone my sinful acts. I'm asking for a new start. Lord, reveal what's the root cause of the offense that continues to prowl my marriages. Remove and heal the sin, Father, in order that I escape death and inherit Your kingdom. Let me become the man you would have me to be. I have failed and made a mess of this marriage and need you to help me. I love my wife. Let me honor and respect her and my children. Please let her be understanding when I tell her what has happened. Please Lord, go before me, and work it all out."*

He positioned himself prostrate at the altar, as the tears flowed down his disappointed face. He kept crying out, *"What's the root cause of the offense that continues to prowl my life?"* After an hour he got quiet and listened to the Lord speak in his heart, *Son it's a generational curse. The spirit of lust and the spirit of rejection live in your heart. Your mother did it to you, and her mother did it to her. Unless you break this, your children are cursed. Your mother was a single parent, and you've felt resented and that you were a burden in her life. The other men in her life always came first. You saw the different men in the household and thought it was okay to have self-gratification.*

After God revealed the answers to him, Steven said, *"Lord, break every curse off me, and release blessings in Jesus name. Amen."*

Son, I forgive you, cleanse you from defilement, and you're healed of all hurts and sin. I bless you. Go speak to your mother today. And go home and talk to Taffi. And sin no more.

Steven answered, *"Lord, I forgive my mother through your grace. But do I have to talk to her about this matter?"*

In order for you to heal, you must speak to your mother today. I want you to go home and talk to Taffi.

He left and went to his mom's house. She was sitting on the porch out, in the coldness, smoking and drinking when he arrived. She had the petite figure of a twenty-year old and wore a pair of tight fitting jeans and a waist-length brown fur coat. She was of Steven's complexion, and her face had aged from the hard life she experienced. Her short gray-streaked hair was in an afro, and it needed combing. He greeted her, and she invited him inside. "How's married life?" she asked in her deep voice.

He sat on the couch and looked uncertain. He began, "That's why I'm here, because I did an unfaithful act that disrespected my wife today. I acted as I did when I was married to Vanessa. At first, I didn't understand what was going on because I love Taffi. She has been a breath of fresh air in my life. I never thought that I would ever hurt her. The root of my problem came after I prayed, and that's why I'm here. I didn't come to condemn you, but to talk." He added with urgency, "I hope you receive what I'm about to say without getting angry. My upbringing has messed me up. I have lacked a sense of belonging because of all the other men in your life. They always came first. I felt resented and as though I was a burden in your life. You saw the different men in our household, and from them you gained self-gratification. You did it, and grandma did it. Mom, you were a single parent, and you conceived me in lust and out of wedlock. From my upbringing, I've become insensitive to the needs of others, angry all the time, abusive and stingy. Today, I received God's grace to love, to forgive you, and to stop every curse of defilement. I'm healed of all the hurts and sin of my past. I hope Taffi will forgive me because she didn't deserve any of this baggage from my past. "

Emma listened as Steven talked. He went all the way back to his childhood. As he talked, the tears began to flow down her face. When he finished, she apologized. She gave him a kiss and said, "You were not a burden to me, but a joy. I'm sorry that I messed up your life from the mess in my life, son. I guess bad practices pass from generation to generation because, what you're telling me, my mom did the same things to me. I promise I'll change my ways. Please forgive me, son."

They hugged for a long time, and he left. When he arrived home, it was around 10:30 P.M., and Taffi was sitting down in the living room relaxing. The kids were asleep. "Where have you been? You didn't have to stay away that long. I've missed you, honey." His heart dropped because he knew she loved him, and this blow could cause it to end.

His voice was calm, "I need to talk to you." She noticed that he had been crying.

She sat by him on the sofa. "Have I done something wrong?"

She studied him, as he said, "No, it isn't you. It's me. I'm the messed up person in this marriage. Before I continue, I want you to know that I love you."

"Okay honey, this is beginning to sound serious. You aren't going to tell me you want a divorce. We haven't even explored marriage and family yet."

He looked down and her heart dropped. He knew he was going into an injurious territory. People's lives would get hurt all because of him and his stupidity. He persevered, feeling as Jesus did when He said, "Father, if you are willing, take this cup from me." His voice paused before he completed his next disclosure, "I hope you have enough love in your heart…."

She felt as though her heart would stop beating as she continued to listen, "…to forgive me for what I'm about to say."

She blew out a breath and placed her finger across his mouth, "Shush! Before you say another word, I want you to know I married you for better or for worst." Steven listened, surprised by her words.

He ignored the fizz of her last encouraging words, and he continued, "You know what type person I've been in the past because I've not kept it a secret. I'm not proud of my past faults or failures. I told you from the beginning that I have problems. I have always loved myself and have been self-centered. I've discovered that I've pampered my faults and failures instead of changing them. The day we left coming back from the honeymoon, I started to have negative feelings about marriage. It was as if I were going back to the times with Vanessa. I felt trapped, living with the children all day." He took hold of her hand, as she hesitated to return the affection. His hands were strong yet tender. "Today, I had the same feelings. Please give me access to your heart of forgiveness for what I'm about to say. I had no intentions of doing wrong, until I went to a car dealership and saw one of my old flings." She felt faint as a tears started to roll down her crimson colored cheek. She turned away.

She felt her heart was going to stop. She laid her head back against the sofa, "Oh no, Steven. . . ." She pulled her hand away from his hand. "No, Steven, we're still in the honeymooning stage."

He demanded, "Hate me, after you hear me out. I don't think I can do this again."

"Why not? You repeat everything else, didn't you?"

Tears flowed down her face. He continued, "Right away I went to your father and spoke to him. He's a man of respectability. He gave me some valuable pointers without even hearing the wrong I did. He told me to repent and to pray to God. I did, in the sanctuary. God ministered to me. The spirit of lust and the spirit of rejection had cursed me for all these years. The Lord revealed the root of my problem—my mom and my upbringing. The Lord blessed me out of every curse today." She narrowed her eyes at him. He continued, "I spoke to my mom, and the meeting went well. We were able to forgive one another." She moved her leg out of a relaxed position. "If you want a divorce, I'll understand, but I want you to know I want to make this marriage work. I feel that I'm able to move on without hurting you any more. I'm healed from my past and able to develop, intimacy, friendship, feelings and love. Please give me a try."

"No, Steven, if I forgive you, when will you take my kindness, and love for granted again? I'm not a doormat—something you step on whenever you get the notion. Next time you'll go all the way. Then what? This whole talk would have been in vain."

"Taffi, I didn't have to tell you my indiscretions, but I wanted to change to be a better man. I love you and want to make this work. Yes, I got my priorities mixed up. But through time I'll get my act together."

"And how long do I have to wait? A lifetime?"

"I'm begging you to forgive me, Taffi." He got on his knees in front of her and continued to beg her for forgiveness. He shed many tears.

The more he begged the more her heart softened. She was still crying, but the tears began to slowly dry up. When she had stopped weeping she looked firm and said, "You hurt me, Steven," as he looked her in the eyes she continued, "Don't ever do it again."

He looked her in her eyes with all sincerity, "I promise, sweetheart, to remain faithful and true. I'm sorry for disrespecting you, Taffi."

"I have vowed to stand by you through thick and thin. This is the thick, and I'll handle this dishonor. I still love you and I'm willing to move on.and pray that nothing else ever happens like this again. Will you promise me that this won't ever happen again in our marriage?"

He held up his fingers, "Scout's honor."

She chuckled, as she shook her head, "No, I want your word of honor."

"I'm glad this is over now versus later." She looked at him, smiled, and gave him a kiss.

After they kissed she walked to the window and said, "Destiny is an everyday leap. Sometimes you make the wrong choices, and it hurts, while destiny finds its way despite the choices you make." As she looked outside the window at the darkness, she saw a glitter of light.

Chapter 14

On the weekend of their six month anniversary, they were going to the mountains to celebrate. Steven had told her what he had planned for the weekend, and it reminded her of Donald.

They decided to let the children stay over Grandma Emma's new home for the weekend. She had become a model grandmother and wanted to make up for all the wrong she'd done to Steven. She started going to church with them. Before long, she gave her life over to Christ. At first, things got worst for her. She hung in there, and now her life had taken a turn for the better. Her finances increased, her attitude changed, she stopped cursing, and smoking, drinking, and her living environment got better. She didn't need a man in her life anymore. She was determined to wait for the Lord to send her the spouse that He wanted her to have, if one at all.

They invited David and Tina to go with them. They were trying to do matchmaking, and it was working wonderfully. David never stopped coming by to visit the kids even after Taffi and Steven married. When David met Tina, he knew she was the one. And Tina had started coming by more when she knew David was around.

They left for the cabin on Friday and weren't due back until Sunday. Steven had planned the weekend to be a vacation made in heaven. When they arrived to the cabin, Taffi and Steven went to their bedroom to put down their suitcases. Steven had ordered bloomed tulips for their bedroom, and David had ordered a bunch for Tina's bedroom. Taffi noticed a note attached to her pillowcase. She opened it, "Honey, I thank you for putting up with me. I'm wishing us many, many, many wonderful years of love together." The whole scenario was something that Donald would've done. She was pleased and happy that Steven was the right man for her.

That night they ate at a diner and went to a movie. The next morning they went horseback riding, hiking and to the pool. By the time they went back to the cabin, everyone was exhausted. The next day Taffi and Steven slept in and had room service for breakfast and for lunch. David and Tina, on the other hand, went into town to eat breakfast, to visit numerous specialty shops, a wax museum, and an amusement park. When they returned around four P.M., the honeymooners were up and waiting for them. They all played mini golf, enjoyed biking, and then ate dinner. At dinner, Taffi noticed that Tina and David looked different. She looked at them as their knotted arms fed each other. Neither said anything.

After dinner, they were to head home. Time had flashed by fast. The weekend had been so enjoyable that no one wanted to make a move. Taffi suggested that they stay one more day, but they couldn't, since Steven had one meeting to attend the next afternoon at work.

As Tina was getting inside the car, David assisted her. He held the door wide open and fell to his knees. He pulled out a teddy bear, and, when she looked inside its stomach, she found a ring. He asked, "Tina will you would marry me?" He placed the ring on her finger as she uttered, "Yes." Taffi and Steven clapped and congratulated them both. They all got in the car and headed home, making wedding plans. As Steven drove, he looked across to Taffi and winked his eye. They all needed this weekend to reunite.

David and Tina decided to get married in a month. Tina wanted sooner, but thought it would interfere with the planning. Tina and Taffi were out everyday getting things for the wedding.

The month passed by fast and before she knew it, Tina was Tina Perry. They had a beautiful wedding at Pine Outreach Center, and Paul Thomas married them.

The next month was quiet because everything had calmed down again. Taffi started to feel sick after she ate in the morning. A couple mornings she barely made it to the bathroom. She and Steven were curious and decided to do a home pregnancy test. They discovered that she was indeed pregnant. They had never discussed having more kids because the understanding was that four was enough. It was a surprise, but they both loved the idea. That night they had agreed to tell the kids the news. When they told the kids, they were disappointed. They didn't want a new baby in the house. After much convincing, they determined it would be nice to have a baby brother. They felt enough girls were in the family, and they needed another boy.

Steven had become interested in Bible study, and Paul Thomas had allowed him to teach on occasion. The day after Steven conducted his second Bible study, he had a dream. He was in a bright illuminated light in an endless place. Radiating from the light was a peace that surpassed all understanding. He heard a voice, *Son, feed my sheep, and Paul Thomas will be your teacher.* He awakened at four A.M. He went into his prayer closet, knelt down on his knees, and started to pray. "God, was this dream real, or was it my imagination? I need to know, Father. "

In his heart, he heard the Holy Spirit say, I'll *confirm your calling today.*

Steven stayed in the closet until about six A.M. He got back in the bed, and as he did, Taffi turned over. He was happy she hadn't stirred because he needed time to think. As he stared at her, he wondered how she would take the news of becoming a pastor's wife. He wanted to wait to get his confirmation before he uttered a word to anybody. He began to twist and turn. He marched into the living room because he didn't want to awaken Taffi. His mind started to think of the negatives. *I can't preach because of my past. How can You ever use me, God? My picture isn't squeaky clean. I'm a sinner that has fallen short of Your glory. I'm not good enough to preach the gospel. I mistreated my first wife and committed adultery while married to her. I've neglected my children. I've lusted after a woman and almost committed adultery on my second wife. You can't use me. I'm messed up, Lord. What do I have to offer Your kingdom? I can't preach because I'm not worthy.*

He felt a wind blow in the room, and he knew it was the presence of the Lord. *Yes, son, I'm capable of using you. You see, I look beyond your faults and see the real you. Your testimonies, along with the Word, will feed my sheep. The day you repented, I forgave you and wiped your record clean. Don't doubt the call on your life because you are worthy.*

Steven fell to his knees and started to praise the Lord. It was 8:00 A.M. when the kids ran into the living room ready to watch television before going to school. He left the room to get ready for work. As he listened to a Christian television station, a pastor caught his attention, and he focused on what he was saying. The pastor said, "God gives many gifts through the Holy Spirit to equip Christians to serve God in the Christian community. Love is a valuable gift. But Ephesians 4:1-13 expounds on five gifts. It was he who gave some to be apostles, some to be prophets, some to be evangelists, and some to be pastors and teachers to prepare God's people for works of service, and the body of Christ will be built up until we all reach unity in the faith and in knowledge of the Son of God and become mature, attaining to the whole measure of the fullness of Christ." The pastor pointed to Steven from the television, "Have you accepted your calling?" He was absorbed in disbelief that the pastor had challenged him with the same interpretation as the dream. After much thought, he realized it wasn't the pastor, but it was God confirming his call to the ministry. He finished getting dressed and went to work. A man stationed outside the church handed him a tracts. Steven took one since they weren't from their church. When he looked at the front of the tract, it unveiled the scripture John 21:15-17. He stopped, and, before entering the church, he read it:

Jesus reinstates Peter. When they had finished eating, Jesus said to Simon Peter, "Simon son of John, do you love me more than these?"

"Yes, Lord," he said, "You know that I love you."

Jesus said, "Feed my lambs."

Again, Jesus said, "Simon son of John, do you love me?"
He answered, "Yes, Lord, you know that I love you."

Jesus said, "Take care of my sheep."

The third time he said to him, "Simon son of John, do you
love me?"

Peter was hurt because Jesus asked him the third time,
"Do you love me?" He said, "Lord, you know all things; you
know that I love you."

Jesus said, "Feed my sheep."

After reading the tract, he knew without a doubt that he
had a calling to feed God's sheep. *Feed my sheep,* kept ringing in
his mind. Inside the sanctuary, he looked back for the man
dispensing the tracts, and he had disappeared. He decided without
a doubt that he would pastor the lost and the hurting by feeding
God's sheep.

He called Taffi and invited her to lunch. She met him at
the restaurant because of errands that had delayed her. Inside she
found him sitting next to a window and staring out as though
confused. At first, he was quiet, it wasn't until after he ate that he
opened up, and disclosed the call on his life to her.

She laughed and explained, "I knew because I had a
dream the night before. I didn't tell you about the dream because
I needed to work some things out within myself. In the dream, I
saw Donald sitting at the right hand of Jesus. Jesus told me that
being a pastor's wife was my destiny, and I needed to obligate
myself to that destiny. He told me I had to say good-bye to my
past. Donald came over to me, blew me a kiss, and waved
goodbye. When I awakened, I knew why Donald had died. I
thought I had got over Donald, but I still held on to a small part
of him in my heart. I've not loved you fully, as I should, because
of my dedication to him. Now, I'm ready to fulfill the destiny
God has for me as a pastor's wife."

Steven was shocked that everything was working out.
When he went back to the office, he told Paul Thomas about the
call on his life. He knew what was going on because the Lord had
spoken to him. Paul Thomas explained what had happened to him
and congratulated him. Paul Thomas suggested he start

instructing the Bible studies. Steven prepared for the next Bible study he would teach.

When the next Wednesday rolled around, Steven chose the topic titled "Are You Blind?" He said, "Turn your Bibles to John 9: 1-9. Jesus is in the city of Jerusalem with his disciples when he sees a man who was blind from birth. The disciples asked whose sin had caused the blindness. They wondered how persons are born with a disability. Jesus said to them neither the man, nor his parents had sinned, nor did a specific sin cause this sickness. The man's problem was in the light of misfortune. It happened in his life in order to display God's work.

"Jesus told them we must do the work of the Father who sent Him. Night is coming, and then no man can work. Jesus said that He is the light of the world in a world of darkness, of evil, sin and ignorance.

"Jesus placed mud made with His saliva on the blind man's eyes. The same substance the man was made of, the dust of the earth. The same used on the potter's wheel. Kneading the clay on the Sabbath was against the law, but Jesus did it and told the blind man, 'Go wash in the pool of Siloam' (meaning Sent). He responded to Jesus and went home seeing. People didn't recognize him as the man that sat and begged. He persisted, 'I am he, the man that sees now.'"

Steven continued, "From this scripture we come to the conclusion that we need to support what God has planned and not question Him. Give God the opportunity to work out your disasters and recognize He brought you out. Don't condemn yourself when healing doesn't come because, when God is ready, it will happen. God is a healer, trust Him and He will fight for you. God loves you, and has a plan for your life.

"There are two types of blindness: Those that are blind to Him and those that lack the ability to physically follow the truth. This message is about coming to accept Jesus as Savior and having faith in Him. Do you see Him, or are you blind to the truth?"

Taffi got Steven's attention and asked to speak. He nodded in approval. She began, "I never questioned God when Esther came down with diabetes. I believed and had the faith that He had healed her. We prayed for healing. Steven, I thank you for that Word because I know I did the right thing. Everybody goes through tests, yet the key is passing the test. Eyes will open and healing occurs when we have faith in God."

Taffi read to the congregation a letter from the Endocrinologist,

Esther James has Type 1 Diabetes Mellitus diagnosed within the past year. Because of this diagnosis, Esther requires close and constant care including insulin injections and blood sugar monitoring at least three times every day.

She stared out at the congregation and said, "With enthusiasm, I report that Esther was taken off the insulin injections yesterday. Her blood sugar levels have been in the normal range of 80 to 120 and no higher. Be faithful to God, and He will return the gesture. God is good, and He heals. Esther is living proof that He's real. Let your eyes be opened to the truth."

Steven smiled at her as she continued, "My father, many years back, explained to me the meaning of Esther's name. He said, 'Her name will be a reminder to you, to her and any future generations to get a whiff of the presence of the almighty King.' I have tried to be faithful to that, even after receiving the bad report. He also said, 'When you stray, the story of Esther will cause you to fall back in line with what's right.' People, God has a plan and a destiny for each of our lives. When I stayed aloof from God's presence, I had no relationship with Him. I did my own thing, lost, with no healing or success. When I tapped into the plan He had predestined, I was able to change the world. Faith is the assurance of things hoped for, the conviction of things not seen. Faith is belief. If we tap into destiny, we'll come out above and not beneath! We'll be healed! And break curses!

"Faith to me defines destiny, which is making it to the finish line. Unbelief causes heartache, wherein belief helps you accomplish a goal. People, God is real and greatly to be praised."

Steven started to clap, and the congregation followed him. He hugged his wife. Taffi whispered in his ear, "You, my love, are a miracle. God has done amazing things in your life. I'm proud of you. Nevertheless, it doesn't end there. Look at my life, my mom's life and your grandmother's life. We have gone through, and the rural roads to destiny weren't easy, but we made it to the finish line and accomplished goals. Sometimes we have to sit back and wait on the Lord to fulfill our outcomes."

At home after the kids had gone to sleep, Steven and Taffi cuddled on the sofa to watch a movie. She had popped some popcorn as they awaited the movie to start at 11:00 P.M., which was within the next fifteen minutes. She turned down the lights and the sound on the television. They loved each other's company. She was so proud of Steven that her words couldn't describe her delight.

As she glanced at him, she said, "I've been thinking, my destiny has been much the same as a two-lane rural road. The roadway's conditions have been challenging. They sometimes contained setbacks—sharp curves, fallen rocks, fallen tree branches, bad lighting or holes that threaten my safety. To be blunt, my destiny hasn't been peaches and cream. I've had some ups that kept me moving on toward my destiny and some downs that delayed it. Sometimes, I've underestimated the risks of rural driving, as with my destiny and the distractions have caused pain."

Steven looked at her and smiled, "Hasn't that happened to us all, particularly me? I thought my life was over and have cried many nights."

She conceded with a smile and said with cheer, "Joking aside, I've experienced...."

He jerked and interjected, "No. I'm the one who has been hurt, and empty inside to the point I thought I would never make it through another day. Infidelity, slothfulness, jail, joblessness, and lust were my entertainment. I'm the one that has incurred damage on my roadways. And what's bad about the whole ordeal, during those times, I couldn't seem to see beyond my problems. After I slowed and steered and focused on the road and not my problems, that's when changes occurred. I've been restored, refreshed, and moving onward."

She reached for a few kernels of popcorn, "Yes, destinies are reachable. I'm living proof of it." After chewing the kernels she continued, "What I've learned is that you win this game if you don't quit or give up. When you quit a painful life, you lose the desire to live as Vanessa did. And that's not an option opened to me."

He agreed and turned away from her to hide the tears running down his face.

She closed her eyes, "I will finish this roller coaster ride because my mission isn't over yet." With her eyes still closed, she reached for his hand and held it tightly. "Sometimes we have to go through rough or hazardous road conditions and endure the bumpy, snake roads to appreciate what life has to offer." Taffi opened her eyes and studied Steven closely, "You could've given up once you went to prison as many people do. Instead, you hung in there and now you are blessed."

He said with a light kindling in his eyes, "It's because of God and you sticking next to me through thick and thin that I've reached my destiny. I can see the sunshine of a brand new day. Honey, my destiny has been a rural roads series of adventures to get to the chapter I'm in now. I've driven up dangerous hills and He has protected me. From the trails I had to endure, He rescued me, and He didn't forget to bless me along the way." They kissed and cuddled a long time, and, when they turned the sound up on the television, half the movie had played. They sat there admiring one another.

Rural Roads Workbook

Objectives

Upon the completion of this workbook, the participants will be able to:

- Identify areas of spiritual strengths and weaknesses in their Christian walk
- Face occurrences that happen in everyday living with biblical armor to defeat the enemy
- Plan and facilitate effective prayer and fasting times
- Recognize areas of strengths and weaknesses concerning other races
- Apply the principles of anti-racism

Directions: Read the three statements below. Decide if the statement is TRUE or FALSE as it relates to you. Circle your response. If you answer FALSE on any question, then continue reading. If you answer TRUE to all three statements, you can go on to the next page.

TRUE   FALSE   1. I know Jesus as my Savior. He's in my heart, and I'm born again.

TRUE   FALSE   2. If I were to die today, I would go to heaven.

TRUE   FALSE   3. I repented of my sins today.

Pause one moment, and focus on the cross. Pause again, and focus on Jesus. Because of your sins, Jesus died on the cross. But He forgives sinners and loves you despite the sin in your life. No one person is perfect we've all sinned and fallen short of His glory.

TRUE   FALSE   4. I would like to receive Jesus as my Lord and Savior.

To be saved isn't hard. All you have to do is <u>repent</u> for your sins first. Say this, "Jesus, forgive me of my sins, wash me, and cleanse me in Jesus Name." Then confess with your mouth, <u>"I believe that Jesus Christ died on the cross, and God raised Him up on the third day with all power in His hands for my sins. Jesus, come into my heart. Fill me with your Holy Spirit in Jesus Name.</u>" Close your eyes, call out, "Jesus, Jesus, Jesus," and feel His presence.

If you repented and confessed, you're saved, and all your sins are forgiven. Get into a Bible believing church that teaches God's Word. Read the Bible daily to learn God's heart and His expectations of you as you walk the Christian walk.

Self-Analysis

Are you growing up in Christ? 1 Peter 2:1-3 states, "Therefore, rid yourselves of all malice and all deceit, hypocrisy, envy, and slander of every kind. Like newborn babies, crave pure spiritual milk, so that by it you may grow up in your salvation, now that you have tasted that the Lord is good." The characteristics below will show if you're growing up in Christ or not. Circle the number that best applies to you on a scale of one to ten. One means I'm doing horrible, whereas a ten means I'm doing excellent. Add one number from each line for a total amount. If you recently confessed Jesus as your Lord and Savior, then do this self-analysis again after two months.

1. I don't just talk-the-talk but I walk-the-walk concerning my
   spirituality. I'm not guilty of breaking the Ten Commandments.
   1   2   3   4   5   6   7   8   9   10

2. I exercise repentance when I sin against God because I fear
   Him.
   1   2   3   4   5   6   7   8   9   10

3. I resist the enemy whenever he's in my presence.
   1   2   3   4   5   6   7   8   9   10

4. I humble myself and fast for a spiritual breakthrough.
   1   2   3   4   5   6   7   8   9   10

5. I allow love to flow throughout the society.
   1   2   3   4   5   6   7   8   9   10

6. I search the Bible and biblical resources for self-improvement
   tactics and I obey them.
   1   2   3   4   5   6   7   8   9   10

7. I respect God enough to spread His Word whenever possible.
   1   2   3   4   5   6   7   8   9   10

8. I give whenever possible without complaining.
   1   2   3   4   5   6   7   8   9   10

9. I pray persistently and put my faith in Jesus Christ.
   1   2   3   4   5   6   7   8   9   10

10. I listen to the Holy Spirit and obey His guidance.
    1   2   3   4   5   6   7   8   9   10

Total = _____

Grading:
Are you a newborn, a child, a teen, or an adult Christian?

{a} 100-90= An adult with excellent strengths
{b} 89-70 = A teen with great strengths but needs some improvements
{c} 69-51= A child with problem areas that need serious readjustments
{d} 50 or below = A newborn with undesirable weaknesses

If you circled fewer than five on any individual characteristic, you are in need of serious improvements

Questions
**The questions below will help you understand this book more.
Do the research in the Bible. You'll find scriptures to refer to
when you need them.**

1. How can you pray and how often?

_____

_____

_____

_____

_____

_____

_____

2. What do you have to do to be saved?

_____

_____

_____

_____

_____

_____

3. What person did Taffi witness to about Christ while in the
   hospital? Should Christians compel people to come to Christ?
   Why?

_____

_____

_____

_____

_____

_____

4. Should we become Christians? What is a Christian?

_____

_____

_____

_____

_____

_____

5. It would have been easier for Taffi to judge Steven for his mistakes in life. Are we to judge one another? Who is the perfect judge?

_____

_____

_____

_____

_____

_____

_____

6. Steven felt that everybody had turned their backs on him but Taffi showed him what?

_____

_____

_____

_____

_____

_____

_____

7. Once you have accepted Christ as your Savior, what other steps are required for a successful everyday Christian lifestyle?

_____

_____

_____

_____

_____

_____

_____

8. How can you become intimate with Christ?

_____

_____

_____

_____

_____

_____

_____

9. Should the color of a person's skin be important? Who showed racism in this book? In other words, are you out in society hating and judging, even if only a select few know of your

racist status? Is God pleased with racism? Are you willing to give up racism?

_____
_____
_____
_____
_____
_____
_____

10. What did Taffi and Esther do before they took Communion?

_____
_____
_____
_____
_____
_____

11. Who got healed of diabetes? What verses do you mediate on for healing? Write them down. If you have a disease, can God heal you?

_____
_____
_____
_____
_____
_____

12. Taffi asked God what she ought to do. Should you ask God what you ought to do in certain situations?

_____
_____
_____
_____
_____
_____

13. Was Steven rejected? What is rejection?

_____
_____

_____
_____
_____
_____
_____

14. How did Vanessa handle the racism when her father confronted her?

_____
_____
_____
_____
_____
_____

15. Many times Taffi showed obedience to God. Do you try to be obedient to God?

_____
_____
_____
_____
_____
_____

16. Is it okay to commit adultery? What is adultery? Have you ever committed adultery? If yes, how did you resolve the situation with God and your spouse?

_____
_____
_____
_____
_____
_____

Answer Key
If you do the research, you'll find more scriptures to add or to refer back to when needed.

1. How can you pray and how often?
    ❖ Pray and talk to God daily.
    ❖ You can pray: *Heavenly Father, Lord, and King, the name above all names, let Your kingdom come and Your will be done on earth as it is in heaven. Give us the food we need. Forgive our wrong deeds. Forgive others doing wrong deeds to us. Keep us from doing wrong.*

2. What do you have to do to be saved?
    ❖ John White was saved when he repented his sins and confessed with his mouth that Jesus Christ is the Son of Man who died on the cross for his sins, and believed in his heart that God raised Him from the dead.
    ❖ Dave was saved by confessing Jesus Christ as Lord.
    ❖ Romans 10:9, 10 (NIV) states, "That if you confess with your mouth, 'Jesus is Lord,' and believe in your heart that God raised him from the dead, you will be saved. For it is with your heart that you believe and are justified, and it is with your mouth that you confess and are saved."

3. What person did Taffi witness to about Christ while in the hospital? Taffi told Vanessa about Christ. Should we compel people to come into Christ? Yes.
    ❖ Every effort is to be made by Christ servant to bring the lost to Him. This is a parable of the Great Banquet it paints a picture of God's abundant provision and invitation of salvation, refused by the Jews, then offered to others not invited.
    Luke14:23-24 (NIV) states, "Then the master told his servant, 'Go out to the roads and country lanes and <u>make them come in</u>, so that my house will be full. I tell you, not one of those men who were invited will get a taste of the banquet.'"
    ❖ Luke19:10 (NIV) states, "For the Son of Man came to seek and to save what was lost."

4. Should we become Christians? Yes. What is a Christian?
    ❖ A Christian is a person committed to Christ. Christianity changes the hearts of men to love one another. It costs us

nothing because Jesus paid the cost so that any one can come to Him. All that is needed is to invite Christ into your life. With Christ comes the promise of eternal life.

❖ Philippians 2:5-7 (NIV) states, "Your attitude should be the same as that of Christ Jesus: Who, being in very nature God, did not consider equality with God something to be grasped, but made himself nothing, taking the very nature of a servant, being made in human likeness."

❖ Luke 14:26-35 (NIV) states, "If anyone comes to me and does not hate his father and mother, his wife and children, his brothers and sisters—yes, even his own life—he cannot be my disciple. And anyone who does not carry his cross and follow me cannot be my disciple.'

"'Suppose one of you wants to build a tower. Will he not first sit down and estimate the cost to see if he has enough money to complete it? For if he lays the foundation and is not able to finish it, everyone who sees it will ridicule him, saying, 'This fellow began to build and was not able to finish.'

"'Or suppose a king is about to go to war against another king. Will he not first sit down and consider whether he is able with ten thousand men to oppose the one coming against him with twenty thousand? If he is not able, he will send a delegation while the other is still a long way off and will ask for terms of peace. In the same way, any of you who does not give up everything he has cannot be my disciple.'

"'Salt is good, but if it loses its saltiness, how can it be made salty again? It is fit neither for the soil nor for the manure pile; it is thrown out.

The underlined short story is about considering the cost before building a tower or placing an army in the field for war. It's a picture of what it would cost before one becomes a Christian."

❖ Acts 11:26 (NIV) states, "The disciples were called Christians first at Antioch."

❖ Acts 26:28, 29 (NIV) states, "Then Agrippa said to Paul, 'Do you think that in such a short time you can persuade me to be a Christian?'
"Paul replied, 'Short time or long—I pray God that not only you but all who are listening to me today may become what I am, except for these chains.'"

❖ 1 Peter 4:16 (NIV) states, "However, if you suffer as a Christian, do not be ashamed, but praise God that you bear that name."

5. It would have been easier for Taffi to judge Steven for his mistakes in life. Are we to judge one another? Who is the perfect judge?
   ❖ No, we are not to judge others.
   ❖ God is the perfect judge therefore; we should not judge one another.
   ❖ Romans 14:10 (NIV) states, "You, then, why do you judge your
   brother? Or why do you look down on your brother? For we will all stand before God's judgment seat."
   ❖ Matthew 7:1 (NIV) states, "Do not judge, or you too will be judged."

6. Steven felt that everybody had turned their backs on him, but Taffi showed him what?
   ❖ Taffi showed him that a person's past didn't end their future and that we should show love for God, not for ourselves.
   ❖ John15:12, 13 (NIV) states, "My command is this: Love each other as I have loved you. Greater love has no one than this, that he lay down his life for his friends."

7. Once you have accepted Christ as your Savior, what other steps are required for a successful everyday Christian lifestyle?
   ❖ Be baptized.
   ❖ Worship Christ.
   ❖ Obey the Ten Commandments.
   ❖ Become intimate with him.
   ❖ Love your neighbor.
   ❖ Attend a church that preaches "Jesus."

8. How can you become intimate with Christ?
   ❖ Prayer and fasting to chat and touch Him builds intimacy.
   ❖ Learning or reading His Word to become familiar with Him brings you closer to Christ.

9. Should the color of a person's skin be important? Who showed racism in this book? Is God pleased with racism?
   ❖ No, the color of a person's skin is not important. Racism is sin.

* Vanessa's father showed racism, along with her mother.
* James 2:1-4 (NIV) states,   "My brothers, as believers in our glorious Lord Jesus Christ, don't show favoritism. Suppose a man comes into your meeting wearing a gold ring and fine clothes, and a poor man in shabby clothes also comes in. If you show special attention to the man wearing fine clothes and say, 'Here's a good seat for you," but say to the poor man, 'You stand there' or 'Sit on the floor by my feet,' have you not discriminated among yourselves and become judges with evil thoughts?"
* Matthew 7:1-2 (NIV) states, "Do not judge, or you too will be judged. For in the same way you judge others, you will be judged, and with the measure you use, it will be measured to you."
* Ephesians 2:14 (NIV) states, "For he himself is our peace, who has made the two one and has destroyed the barrier, the dividing wall of hostility."
* Matthew 22:39 (NIV) states, "And the second is like it; 'Love your neighbor as yourself.'"
* Galatians 5:14 (NIV) states, "The entire law is summed up in a single command: "Love your neighbor as yourself."
* Luke 10:30-37 (NIV) states, "In reply Jesus said: 'A man was going down from Jerusalem to Jericho, when he fell into the hands of robbers. They stripped him of his clothes, beat him and went away, leaving him half dead. A priest happened to be going down the same road, and when he saw the man, he passed by on the other side. So too, a Levite, when he came to the place and saw him, passed by on the other side. But a Samaritan, as he traveled, came where the man was; and when he saw him, he took pity on him. He went to him and bandaged his wounds, pouring on oil and wine. Then he put the man on his own donkey, took him to an inn and took care of him. The next day he took out two silver coins and gave them to the innkeeper. Look after him,' he said, 'and when I return, I will reimburse you for any extra expense you may have.'

    "Which of these three do you think was a neighbor to the man who fell into the hands of robbers?

    "The expert in the law replied, 'The one who had mercy on him.'

    "Jesus told him, 'Go and do likewise.'"

❖ 1 Corinthians 13:1 (NIV) states, "If I speak in the tongues of men and of angels, but have not love, I am only resounding gong or a clanging cymbal."

❖ Leviticus 19:18 (NIV) states, "'Do not seek revenge or bear a grudge against one of your people, but love your neighbor as yourself. I am the LORD.'"

10. What did Taffi and Esther do before they took Communion?

❖ They prayed for Esther's healing and examined themselves to be sure that they were living according to the Word.

❖ 1 Corinthians 11:23-30 (NIV) states, "For I received from the Lord what I also passed on to you: The Lord Jesus, on the night he was betrayed, took bread, and when he had given thanks, he broke it and said, 'This is my body, which is for you; do this in remembrance of me.' In the same way, after supper he took the cup, saying, 'This cup is the new covenant in my blood; do this, whenever you drink it, in remembrance of me.' For whenever you eat this bread and drink this cup, you proclaim the Lord's death until he comes.

"Therefore, whoever eats the bread or drinks the cup of the Lord in an unworthy manner will be guilty of sinning against the body and blood of the Lord. A man ought to examine himself before he eats of the bread and drinks of the cup. For anyone who eats and drinks without recognizing the body of the Lord eats and drinks judgment on himself. That is why many among you are weak and sick, and a number of you have fallen asleep."

11. Who got healed of diabetes? What verses to mediate on for healing? Can God heal?

❖ Esther was healed of diabetes.

❖ Luke 6:18, 19 (NIV) states, "Who had come to hear him and to be healed of their diseases. Those troubled by evil spirits were cured, and the people all tried to touch him, because power was coming from him and healing them all."

❖ Isaiah 53:4 (NIV) states, "Surely he took up our infirmities and carried our sorrows, yet we considered him stricken by God, smitten by him, and afflicted."

❖ Matthew 8:17 (NIV) states, "He took up our infirmities and carried our diseases."

❖ Mark 11:23, 24 (NIV) states," I tell you the truth, if anyone says to this mountain, 'Go, throw yourself into the sea,' and does not doubt in his heart but believes that what he says will happen, it will be done for him."

❖ 2 Corinthians 10:4, 5 (NIV) states, "The weapons we fight with are not the weapons of the world. On the contrary, they have divine power to demolish strongholds. We demolish arguments and every pretension that sets itself up against the knowledge of God, and we take captive every thought to make it obedient to Christ."

12. Should you ask God what you ought to do in certain situations?

❖ Psalm 91:2 (NIV) states, "I will say of the Lord, 'He is my refuge and my fortress, my God, in whom I trust.'"

❖ John 16:13 (NIV) states, "But when he, the Spirit of truth, comes, he will guide you into all truth. He will not speak on his own; he will speak only what he hears, and he will tell you what is yet to come."

13. Was Steven rejected? What is rejection?

❖ Yes, Steven was rejected when he tried to obtain employment after imprisonment.

❖ His mother also rejected him, and it caused him to have problems in his life.

❖ Rejection is a feeling that many people conform to when discarded by others.

❖ Psalms 27:10 (NIV) states, "Though my father and mother forsake me, the Lord will receive me."

14. How did Vanessa handle the racism when her father confronted her?

❖ Vanessa left the same day that he confronted, her and she married Steven the next day.

15. Should we be obedient to God?

❖ Exodus 23:22, 23 (NIV) states, "If you listen carefully to what he says and do all that I say, I will be an enemy to your enemies and will oppose those who oppose you. My angel will go ahead of you."

❖ Jeremiah 42:6 (NIV) states, "Whether it is favorable or unfavorable, we will obey the Lord our God, to whom we are sending you, so that it will go well with us, for we will obey the Lord our God."

❖ Isaiah 1:19 (NIV) states, "If you are willing and obedient, you will eat the best from the land; but if you resist and rebel, you will be devoured by the sword."

16. Is it okay to commit adultery? What is adultery?
 ❖ No, it is not okay to commit adultery.
 ❖ Adultery is a sinful act of unfaithfulness within a covenant relationship with a spouse.
 ❖ Exodus 20:14 (NIV) states, "You shall not commit adultery is one of the Ten Commandments that God gave to Moses on Mount Sinai."
 ❖ Proverbs 6:25-29 (NIV) states, "Do not lust in your heart after her beauty or let her captivate   you with her eyes, for the prostitute reduces you to a loaf of bread, and the adulteress preys upon your very life.

  "Can a man scoop fire into his lap without his clothes being burned?

  "Can a man walk on hot coals without his feet being scorched?

  "So is he who sleeps with another man's wife; no one who touches her will go unpunished."
 ❖ Matthew 5:27-28 (NIV) states, "You have heard that it was said, 'Do not commit adultery.' But I tell you that anyone who looks at a woman lustfully has already committed adultery with her in his heart."

Racism Test

What is your relationship with people from other races? This test will answer that question. Note: Each row is numbered. Circle the response that most nearly relates to your thinking or behavior pattern in each row. Then go to the next numbered row. Once the test is completed, copy your answers to the answer key found on the next page.

1.I think God loves only my race	1.I think God loves all races	1.I think God sometimes loves other races
2.I prefer to be around all races	2.I prefer to be around one other race	2.I prefer to be around only my race
3.I only love other races when I'm in the mood for them	3.I'll never love other races	3.I love other races
4.I'll never stand up for other races	4. I stand up for other races	4.I sometimes stand up for other races
5.I stereotype other races	5.I sometimes stereotype other races	5.I never stereotype other races
6.I think only my race is active	6.I sometimes think other races are lazy	6.I never think other races are lazy
7.I always generalize negative traits about other races	7.I sometimes generalize negative traits about other races	7.I never generalize negative traits about other races
8.I lack confidence in other races	8.I sometimes trust other races	8.I trust other races
9.I care about other races	9.I don't care about other races	9.I sometimes care about other races
10.If I were a manager, I would hire a variety of people from other races	10.If I were a manager, I would hire only 1or 2 people outside my race	10.If I were a manager, I would never hire people outside my race

Racism Test Answer Key
Transcribe your answers from the Racism Test to the appropriate answers found under the three bold printed columns: **Excellent Behavior**, **Needs Improvement**, or **Racist???**

Excellent Behavior (+10)	Needs Improvement (+5)	Racist??? (-10)
1. I think God love all races	1.I think God sometimes loves other races	1.I think God loves only my race
2.I prefer to be around all races	2.I prefer to be around one other race	2.I prefer to be around only my race
3.I love other races	3.I only love other races when I'm in the mood for them	3.I'll never love other races
4.I stand up for other races	4.I sometimes stand up for other races	4.I'll never stand up for other race
5.I never stereotype other races	5.I sometimes stereotype other races	5.I stereotype other races
6.I never think other races are lazy	6.I sometimes think other races are lazy	6.I think only my race is active
7.I never generalize negative traits about other races	7.I sometimes generalize negative traits about other races	7.I always generalize negative traits about other races
8.I trust other races	8.I sometimes trust other races	8.I lack confidence in others races
9.I care about other races	9.I sometimes care about other races	9.I don't care about other races
10.If I were a manager, I would hire a variety of people from other races	10.If I were a manager, I would hire only 1 or 2 people outside my race	10.If I were a manager, I would never hire people outside my race
Total: (+)	Total: (+)	Total: (-)
		Racism Score Total=

Racism Score

The circled behaviors on the Racism Test Answer Key on the previous page reveal your relationship with other races. Each column has a number assigned to it. In the **Excellent Behavior** column, add ten points for each circled behavior. Place the total at the bottom of that column. In the **Needs Improvement** column, add five points for each circled behavior. Place the total at the bottom of that column. In the **Racist???** column, subtract ten points for each circled behavior. Place the total at the bottom of that column. After adding, the first two columns totals, and subtracting the last column total, you have a **Racism Score Total**.

Check your status below:
{a} 100-90= Excellent strengths.
{b} 89-70 = Some strengths, but need some improvements.
{c} 69-51= Problem areas that needs improvements.
{d} 50 or below = Undesirable weaknesses that need immediate attention!

If you find any circled responses under the **Needs Improvement** or the **Racist???**, columns or a score of 89 or below then you've detected problem areas. The next step is going to work on changing your sinful nature. Correct the bad behavior by having a friend sign the Anti-Racism Supporters Contract with you. Become accountable for racist behavior!

Anti-Racism Supporters Contract
Directions: Pick a dedicated person to sign this contract. Sometimes you need a support partner to be there for encouragement. For a true revelation, have the supporter be a person from another race.

Anti-Racism Supporters Contract

I, _____, promise to be a supporter to_____, during his/her time of changing racist behavior. I promise not to be a hindrance but a true friend who's not afraid to speak out when he/she is wrong. Strength comes in numbers, and I promise to be your strength in time of need.

Supporter   signature:
_____

Date:_____

Anti-Racism Contract
Directions: Make a contract with yourself. This contract is a tool that may motivate you to change by binding you to make changes, in other words, to make a commitment. Are you game enough to try this contract?

Anti-Racism Contract

I, _____, agree to make an effort this week to stop my racist behavior towards people of different races. I agree to be honest and truthful to myself about these inappropriate behaviors. If I do wrong, I will rectify my mistakes as soon as possible. I'll pay close attention to my interaction, thoughts, speech, and attitude. If I find my behavior inappropriate towards a person, I'll change immediately by doing something nice for the person I've offended within the week. I know that my success is totally up to "me." This works . . . if I'll work. I'm a special person, grafted into the olive tree; therefore, I have the power to control my actions toward others.

Signature:_____

Date:_____

The purpose of this contact is to motivate me to change
my racist behavior. This contract holds me
accountable for my own actions.

Prayer Contract
Directions: Make a contract with yourself. This contract is a tool that may motivate you to increase your prayer time by binding you to make prayer a priority. If you feel this tool will work for you, use it.

Prayer Contract

I, _____, agree to make prayer a daily occurrence. I understand this is an effective way of communicating with Christ. I'll make time to touch Jesus whenever possible throughout my day. I know my success is up to me.

Signature: _____

Date: _____

Prayer Achievement
Goal: Your goal is to stay focused on the Lord long enough to increase your prayer time to <u>numerous times</u> throughout your busy <u>day</u>. Do you have to pray in your prayer closet? If possible, go to your prayer closet. However, you can pray anywhere and at anytime. It's easy. While you're in your car; in the elevator; in the grocery line; waiting at your doctor's office; while exercising, focus on Jesus, and start speaking to Him. If people are around, pray to the Lord in your mind. Be creative as to where to sneak in a prayer or two. Prayer times may change until you reach at least <u>numerous times a day</u>. (Psalms 55:22)

I have increased my weekly prayer time from _____ days per week to _____days per week.
Date of change: _____.
Start date: _____.

Fasting Achievement
Goals: Fasting is self-denial. Are you fasting? The key is to increase the times you fast. Fasting should become part of your spiritual walk. Fasting brings you closer to the Lord by increasing your faith. It helps you overcome the enemy. And it disciplines a Christian. The Holy Spirit will lead, guide, and direct you when to fast. During those times, be obedient to the Spirit. (Isaiah 58) (Matthew 6:17-21).

I fasted _____days this month.
Month: _____.

Printed in the United States
56011LVS00006B/499-519

9 780977 703425